Negras

SUNDIAL HOUSE

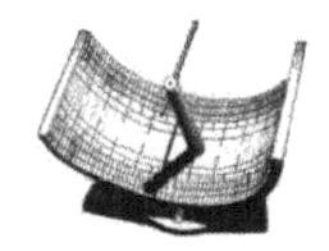

Negras

Bilingual Edition

Yolanda Arroyo Pizarro

Translated by

Alejandro Álvarez Nieves

SUNDIAL HOUSE NEW YORK • PHILADELPHIA

First paperback edition: October 2022

Book design by Lisa Hamm
Cover image by Scherezade García: "Stories of Wonder," from the series of *Early Encounters* (2019). Acrylic, pigment, charcoal and spray on canvas, 72 x 48 inches. Private Collection.
Photography by William Vázquez.
Proofreading by Lizdanelly López Chiclana

ISBN: 979-8-9879264-2-0 (paperback)

Contents

The Kingdom

Of this World

Contenido

(las) Negras

El Reino

De este mundo

Writing (*las*) *Negras*

YOLANDA ARROYO PIZARRO

TRANSLATED BY ALEJANDRO ÁLVAREZ NIEVES

Slaves were very happy.
They were very happy people being slaves.

THESE WERE the first lines I learned in the third grade from our History and Social Studies teacher, Sister Rosario. The nun apparently needed us to learn this brainwashed mantra at any cost because she made us recite it by heart, at least me and Juan Carlos, the other Black child in the classroom. We were made an example; we were chosen so that the rest of the children of Cataño, with lighter skin, whiter skin, clearer skin, not as black as us, could understand that the myth of the three races in Puerto Rico was not as much a myth after all. It was real, and, aside from deifying yourself by assuming a white, Spanish identity (according to this nun), and aside from haughtingly recognizing yourself as a brown-skinned

Taino with straight hair (according to this nun), we had to feel as much as or even more pride—never superiority—for being descendants of Black African slaves with bad hair (according to this nun).

Yet I was the *daughter* of my grandmother, Petronila, a being like no other, who bore a subversive granddaughter, defying biology, mother nature, and deities of any kind. The upbringing my *abuela* provided created a being that would refute everything that stood in her path until her most polemic questions were addressed. "You are a spirit of contradiction," abuela Petronila would vociferate, upset as she would run after me among the chickens and roosters in the yard of our house in a neighborhood called Amelia. She almost always bragged about me, yet she would become exasperated from time to time, as her own creation occasionally conspired against her. "You never remain silent, you are contentious. Your mouth brims with insolence. This shall be your undoing," she would rebuke her Opera Prima.

Abuela Toní—short for Petronila Cartagena Mitchen, born on December 5, 1912—expressed any statement in the most intelligent and brilliant way, never before witnessed by me. She learned Spanish by reading *Enciclopedia Cumbre* and conversational English at school, up to the eight grade. She knew how to instill and persuade, enough to become a secretary at Puerto Rico Cement until the most charming consort in town appeared, my grandfather, Saturnino Pizarro Costoso.

With such a lush, hypnotizing eloquence, she would defend her ideas, would assuage disputes, would refute opinions about the past and the future of the archipelago, would admonish the other matriarchs on calle Herminio Díaz Navarro, and would organize neighborhood conspiracies to survive hurricanes as soon as the seawall waves swept in from the bay. She compared hurricanes Hugo and David with hurricane San Ciriaco in 1899, whose details she knew well thanks to the stories of ancestress Georgina, her mother, my great grandmother.

I coined the word "ancestress"[1] while writing short stories in a trance. It was 1998, and I was pregnant with Aurora, my only daughter. I was writing to reminisce about *abuela* Petronila, to rescue her, to embrace her, as Alzheimer threatened to spirit her away. I came up with "ancestress" to talk about my *abuelas*, my great grandmothers, and my great-great grandmothers. I already had experience with made-up words, for Petronila already said "desosirium."[2] Miguelina, my paternal grandmother, spoke a little German in addition to English and Spanish, and this skill forced her to "Creolize" some expressions; that is, to create a way for us to understand each other. Other madame grandmothers from the neighborhood, immigrants from smaller Caribbean islands, spoke to me in French, Creole, and Swahili. Therefore, the combination of verb tenses, impossible conjugations, and the birth of neologisms always came naturally to me.

Thus, when I sat down at three in the morning to write down the first paragraph of *las Negras* in 2003, I knew I had to emphasize the feminine in Blackness. I knew that I wanted the title of my book to begin with the article in lower case, followed by the noun in upper case.[3] I wanted the adjectivization of that noun, or the nominalization of that adjective, to become a protagonist. A dark *prietagonista*. For this reason, in 2003, bearing the pain of my abuela-madre's death, I had no escape but to enter into a trance . . . writing the stories that Petronila had told me, listening to the words from the women of my lineage though the voice of Mami Toní.

I cherish the image of my grandmother telling these stories about her own grandmothers. Negras who came in by boat, Negras who worked the land, Negras who became midwives, Negras who paved the roads, who were punished, reprimanded, who took revenge, who poisoned their captors. Abuela would dictate words to me while she was alive, present, in flesh and bone, and after she passed away she also dictated words to me in my dreams, in my memories, in my hallucinations, because I hallucinated as I wept, as I yearned for her, as I missed her.

Therefore, on that day in 1978 when a nun showed me a picture of a smiling Taíno and a dashing Spanish conquistador next to a "happy" African, an image we had been "learning" for weeks as part of our island's history, I invoked my "spirit of contradiction" and haughtily declared, Petronila style, "No chained person can be happy." Immediately the room burst in raucous laughter, which concluded with my visit to the principal's office at Colegio San Vicente Ferrer. Sister Soledad recommended that I write on the blackboard, in cursive, a cautionary sentence as foolproof punishment, in front of the entire class: "I must respect authority." And so I did. I wrote on the green board with white chalk, in perfect penmanship, while I recited the words, "my authority is *abuela* Petronila."

No chained person can be happy. Hence, as I assert my free will, I embody my abuela-madre every time I please, every time I dream her, every time I conjure her, every time I write her. Every time you read *Negras*.

Notes

1 The author claims coinage of the word "ancestra." The final -a is a gender morpheme indicating a female ancestor, as opposed to "ancestor," whose final -o indicates male or neutral. I played with the same analogy with ancestor-ancestress, as the morpheme *-tor* is male in Latin and can be opposed to a female morpheme, *-tress*. [T.N.]

2 According to the author, this word is the combination of *desolación* and *delirio*, which I render in English as *desosirium* (desolation + delirium). [T.N.]

3 Thus, contrary to Spanish capitalization norms. [T.N.]

Translator's Note

ALEJANDRO ÁLVAREZ NIEVES

A RENDERING born out of love. This project was a happy accident. Yolanda had just been selected for the prestigious Bogotá 39 list of Latin American authors with her first book, *Ojo de Luna*. While collaborating as curator for Mayra Santos-Febres' Festival de la Palabra, I received a copy of *las Negras* in 2012. The book went straight to the books-to-read pile, and there it stayed for a few of weeks. Until it finally reached my hands. I saw the connection with English-speaking Black writers immediately—Morrison, Danticat, Lorde, Angelou, Shange, just to name a few. It became clear to me that this work had to be available in English. So, I asked permission to translate the book. Yolanda generously accepted. It took me about a month to complete the translation. The working title was to be *Negras: Stories of Black Puerto Rican Women*. At that time, there was no need for me to charge anything. I was completing my dissertation. The joy and personal peace I received from this privilege was enough. Thus, life continued its path. Yolanda went on to become one of Puerto Rico's most prominent writers. I continued teaching, translating, and organizing a festival. In 2019 I received an email from Sundial House's editor, Eunice Rodríguez Ferguson. She wanted to commission my services for a new edition of *las Negras*. My condition was that Yolanda had to agree to engage me as her translator. She accepted. I was honored. There were many other options for a translator, especially ten years after the original publication. Especially after how much the world has changed in a decade regarding Black rights. Today it is my pleasure to work with Yolanda once again. In the end, translation is a linguistic skill rooted in words. My love for Yolanda Arroyo-Pizarro and her work are deeply embedded within this new English version.

If there are two main challenges in rendering Yolanda's prose into English, one could argue for the main title and the use of verb tenses. The first time around, it was evident to me that keeping the source text's wording in English would not favor the intent of the author. The definite article *la* introduces a category for generic use which English just does not tend to use. The female morpheme *-a*, combined with the article would be something like "The Black Women," or even "Those Black Women"; hence, my first option answered to an explanatory approach. There is not much literature about Black women from or coming to Puerto Rico, or about their ancestors, in Spanish, even less in English. Also, the word *black* had yet to be widely used in upper case to refer to origin and culture of a people. It was clear to me that Arroyo-Pizarro's work relies on brevity, yet I did not want to give the impression that the women in this book were to be stereotyped or misconceived. This book is about starting a dialogue about rewriting Blackness, and therefore retelling the history of Black women that were taken by force from their home and brought over to Puerto Rico, or at least captured to be taken to the island. Since the first story is about a Black warrior captured with the intent of taking her to the Caribbean yet does not live the Puerto Rican experience, so we resolved to leave the title in Spanish—*Negras*. I believe keeping the name in Spanish without the article precisely starts the desired dialogue in the generic use intended by Arroyo-Pizarro. That female *-a* is the beginning of conversation with all Black English-speaking women who descend from the same tradition. It is a linguistic invitation to sisterhood.

As other Caribbean writers, Yolanda Arroyo-Pizarro works on revealing just enough by using verb tenses and complex syntax. The use of the present tense in contrast with the past creates a desired effect that is not easy to pull off in Spanish. Fortunately, with the rise of memoirs and chronicles as a literary genre, Arroyo-Pizarro's style has endured the test of time. In English, fellow Caribbean writers like Marlon James and Edwidge Danticat also alternate verb tenses with mastery. Therefore, I did my best to maintain verb tenses in favor of an effect whenever possible. Arroyo-Pizarro is a very visual writer. She tends to focus on a detail like looking into a microscope, only to widen the lens like a telescope. One of her mechanisms is to alter the syntax, a feat more possible in Spanish as verbs have flexion to refer to grammatical person. I maintained the order whenever I could so readers can appreciate the way she constructs her stories.

Yolanda's poems, selected here from *Yo, Makandal (I, Makandal)* are a challenge as they are infused with Puerto Rican references. One of the main decisions was to maintain the Yoruba names of deities as they are written correctly in English. Yoruba as a spoken language is mainly circumscribed to some communities in Cuba, therefore, there is no correct way to spell out names. One just writes the word as you hear it, which is the spelling rule in Spanish. This means that there are no standardized ways to write the names of the *òrìṣàs*, which are commonly written as *orishas*. I decided to keep the Nigerian Yoruba spelling because this is the way in which the practitioners of Osha, more commonly known as Santería or Lucumí religion, write the names of the *òrìṣàs*. Once can see *Ọṣun*, the deity of fertility and communication, represented by the river, spelled in Spanish as *Ochún* or *Ochun* or *Oshún* or *Oshún*. Using the correct Nigerian spelling, as some priests and priestesses of Santería in Puerto Rico do, provides a uniform way of spelling. In addition, it evokes the original aspect of the religion, which today is practiced slightly differently in Nigeria and Black Latin America. Be that as it may, I wanted her work to evoke ancestry, which is what the purpose of the selected poems.

The case of *la babalao* followed the same reasoning. Babalawos are the highest-ranking priests in Santería. Following a syncretism with Catholicism, mainly to avoid the Inquisition, women are not allowed to become babalawos, as the word itself is reserved for males—*babá* (father) *lawo* (of paths). In some parts of Nigeria today, however, although not recognized by the Lucumí tradition (the dominant denomination in the Americas) women are allowed to become *iyalawos—iyá* (mother) *lawo* (of paths). I preferred to use the female name in Yoruba because the article in English cannot express gender, as *la* in Spanish does.

The poems referred to above, translated as "God Save Thee, Yemọja," is formatted as the Rosary Prayer. One of the main intentions of *I, Makandal* as a book is to rewrite traditional Catholic prayers as chants for Black, Puerto Rican women. Thus, I researched these prayers in English and kept the corresponding format. Such a structure sometimes required to prefer the form to the sense.

Another strong poetic current of Yolanda's work is romantic poems for other women. In my opinion, these are her very best, and there were some real challenges regarding Puerto Rico's colloquial lexicon. One such work is *parejera,* used in Puerto Rico to mean "arrogant" or "haughty," even "confrontational," especially used pejoratively against Black women. I decided to keep the word in Spanish in order to reveal this appropriation by the author. Another word I kept in Spanish was *bembe* or *bemba,* used in some regions derisively to refer to thick lips, especially regarding a Black person. Again, I believe Arroyo-Pizarro is reappropriating these slurs as her own.

I ultimately hope that Yolanda Arroyo-Pizarro's persona as a Black writer is manifest in these pages. Her writing is direct, concise, and powerful, exactly like her. It is my professional understanding that Arroyo-Pizarro's prose and poetry communicate extremely well with Black literature written by and for women. Each story or poem is a retelling of several aspects that must come to light in these times. As Ntozake Shange confided in me once as her translator, "I want my work in Spanish because I know there are other places besides America where enslaved African women were brought by force. I want them to them to know my story." My hope is that this English version of Yolanda's work becomes part of the conversation, providing a revealing verse and prose that carries these knowledges further. My friend, the late Zake is in these stories, and so is my great grandmother, as one of the many *Negras* that came before us and comprise our ancestry.

The Negras We Are

ODETTE CASAMAYOR

TRANSLATED BY ALEJANDRA C. QUINTANA AROCHO

WHO ARE WE, Black women of the Americas? To whom do we ascribe our present? Who fostered our existence? Where may we find our mothers? How may we recover their shrouded yet unassailable legacy? For we feel them—robust—on our backs, infusing our voices with their breath. For we know we owe our survival to our mothers and grandmothers, and their mothers and grandmothers. We owe it to them and to the unutterable number of women kidnapped in Africa, deprived of their humanity and exported as instruments of labor to the Americas. We seek the mothers effaced by pages of written history. Effaced by those who engaged in a zealous quest to perpetuate the same order and the same power that have sustained centuries of unrelenting coloniality.

It is to the "the historians, for leaving us out" that Yolanda Arroyo Pizarro dedicates *las Negras*. She is cognizant that the stories of Wanwe, Ndizi, Tshanwe, and Petra burst into and fill historical lacunae that have been deliberately ignored.

From the "demonic ground" incisively identified by Sylvia Wynter[1] as the spaces of the imaginary of exclusion to which we are relegated as Black women, our protagonists emerge to relate the silenced enslaved experience, exerting the agency we have been denied for centuries.

"Here we are again . . . bodies present," the author continues to proclaim. For she recurs to the flesh and the body to better reconstruct the blurry narratives of their lives. The historical archives, rigorously consulted in her writing of *las Negras*, may have offered Yolanda clues regarding the existence of these women, but they will never suffice. The Black women that appear in these archives are "spectacularly violated, objectified, disposable, hypersexualized, and silenced."[2] They evince the exterminating violence that laid waste to their bodies and continues to silence their voices in documents that are traditionally consulted for the production of history.

As *cimarrona* as her characters, Yolanda inveighs against the "epistemic violence" that permeates the archives and reaches an understanding of who the enslaved women were and who we, as their descendants, are today. If we have no trustworthy data to rely upon, if the agency of enslaved women has not been recorded or even afforded thorough attention, if their testimonies were potentially twisted to fit narratives foreign to their own, we have our flesh, which revolts and reveals the ineffable experience.

Yolanda's path reflects the journey that many of us Black women have embarked upon in search of our origins. It is the journey Saidiya Hartman recounted in *Lose your Mother,* set on surveying "an itinerary of destruction from the coast to the savanna," excavating the wounds of our enslaved ancestors.[3] Once in Ghana, she continued to ask herself if there truly was a place in the world that could "sate four hundred years of yearning for a home."[4] Our home is not found here or there. Our home is not in the Americas or in Europe, where our bodies are subdued by alterity and our experience is structurally silenced. Our home is not in Africa, where the same bodies and the same history are also ignored—for being absent, forgotten, and never appropriately memorialized. It is elusive, this home of ours; a home that we sometimes imagine in the middle of the ocean, unreachable. "We have no ancestry except the black water and the Door of No Return," Dionne Brand wrote, also attempting to solve the "existential dilemma" of Afrodescendants.[5]

The traces of our past thus seem irretrievable, but we uphold the belief that this is not the case. Somewhere, they await us. "I think Blacks in the Diaspora carry the Door of No Return in our senses,"[6] it became clear to Brand; and also to Hartman that "[w]e may have forgotten our country, but we haven't forgotten our dispossession."[7] Yolanda Arroyo Pizarro asserts this belief when, in *las Negras,* she invites us on a similar voyage. The trajectory, however, does not push our bodies far enough. This voyage does not lead our bodies to cross the Atlantic and to blend among crowds that, despite sharing the colors and the texture of our skins, we fail to fully recognize—and who do not recognize us completely either. To re-encounter the women of our past, Yolanda does not propose a physical journey. She only urges us to inhabit the flesh of Wanwe, Ndizi, Tshanwe, and Petra.

As such, in Yolanda's prose, the brutality of the Transatlantic slave trade and the processes of enslavement are the pus and blood leaking from the wounds of her characters. Everything is mediated through the captives' bodily sensations. The panic and uncertainty of the African woman who has yet to understand what her kidnapping and transplantation to inconceivable destinations will entail, after traversing an ocean hitherto unknown, spill over into her bewilderment as she hears the commotion of incomprehensible languages, the silence and the cries. A cacophony of sorrow inside the hold of the slave ship becomes indistinguishable from her own. It intertwines with the pestilence and secretions of that jumble of flesh to which she now unwittingly belongs. The forced conversion of Wanwe, the protagonist of our first story: the destruction of her humanity and the inception of her American identity, as merchandise, is not a concept fully broached in inchoate attempts to explain the Black experience with academically legitimized methodologies. For Wanwe and for the readers whom Yolanda's words reach, enslavement does not constitute an abstract process; it is a lived experience. In the flesh of the protagonists of the three other stories, Ndizi, Tshanwe, and Petra, in which enslavement has been accomplished already, the process is marked by the pain of relentless torture and rape.

Yolanda endeavors to remind us that the historicization of the Afrodescendant experience should not begin with the customary retelling of the Transatlantic slave trade. The vessels in which enslaved peoples were transported to the Americas are too often chosen as the symbolic origin of the Afrodescendant's history. Even though a new non-existence as beasts of burden is imposed on Africans from the very moment of their capture, their existence and that of their descendants did not start during the sinister enslavement enterprise.

Wanwe begins her tale by proclaiming that her first memory might be that of the ship she was pushed into in Africa, but her mind immediately wanders into the past, undoing her journey of dispossession. Mentally returning to her childhood village, she recovers the humanity stolen from her, regardless of the chains that brand her enslaved condition at this time in her story. Through the African memories of Wanwe, Tshanwe, and Ndizi, conceptions of a world different than the one imposed on them are evoked and acknowledged, not only within the tales but also in the history of Afrodescendants. As the heroines of *las Negras* demonstrate, our ancestors brought with them knowledge inaccessible to their oppressors. Our ancestors deployed that wisdom to resist annihilation and dehumanization. If they had learned the art of traditional medicine in Africa, they would resort to this knowledge in the Americas. Through abortion and infanticide, they could keep the children of enslaved women from suffering their mothers' fate, while also depriving slave owners of their capital. If they had been warriors and strategists before, once enslaved, they could exploit the hubris of slave owners to escape to the marsh and fling deadly arrows from there. They were aware of the power they secretly still held: "The problem of those who oppress, [. . .] is not oppression itself, but rather the underestimation of the oppressed. [. . .] Now we are encouraged not to defend ourselves because we belong to a master. Oppressors have such liberties, yet they underestimate us," Ndizi warns the friar that seeks her confession.

Yolanda Arroyo Pizarro knows that enduring transgenerational threads are interwoven between her flesh and that of her protagonists. Regardless of the centuries that separate the experience of our enslaved ancestors and ours, the pain and oppression persist, as Black women are systematically saddled with all-encompassing otherness. Because she can feel it as her own, Yolanda makes effective use of that connection to sew the narrative of the Black flesh, wounded and hurting. Flesh that is also rebellious, for to render a phenomenological recreation of the cruel dispossession of humanity that enslaved women endured is only one of her objectives in *las Negras*.

In these pages, the *cimarrón* cry resonates far more forcefully than any cry of lament. The protagonists actively dissent from their condition as slaves and, more importantly, from their condition as *negras*—as an identity constructed by and under Eurocentric epistemology. *Negras* are no longer *negras* because only they can know and affirm who they really are. Despite the slave owners' initials, perennially branded on their flesh with a blazing iron, there will be no way to identify them, unless they have a say. Only then will they also cease to be "the others." In their self-conception they do not render themselves under the categories fabricated by their oppressors, but rather through their own sense of belonging and their vision of the world.

Theirs are thus different epistemologies because they are forged by women who are more than *negras*. These women have engendered themselves. They can be considered socially dead from the perspective of the society that alienates them, but they do not see themselves as inexistent or helpless at all. They inhabit—and define—another time and space. These are the spaces of the marsh they escape to and the memory of African life before the kidnapping and transplantation to the Americas. They reaffirm that *cimarronaje* is more than just about the mere escape. Having undone her chains, the *cimarrona* is also the procreator of her own self, once she decides who she wants to be and how she wants to act, where to be and what to think.

Moreover, I return to the initial questions: Who are we, Black women of the Americas? Silence and monstrosity usually cast a shadow over every answer. They haunt us, for instance, when we are called upon to remember the tortured face of Anastácia.

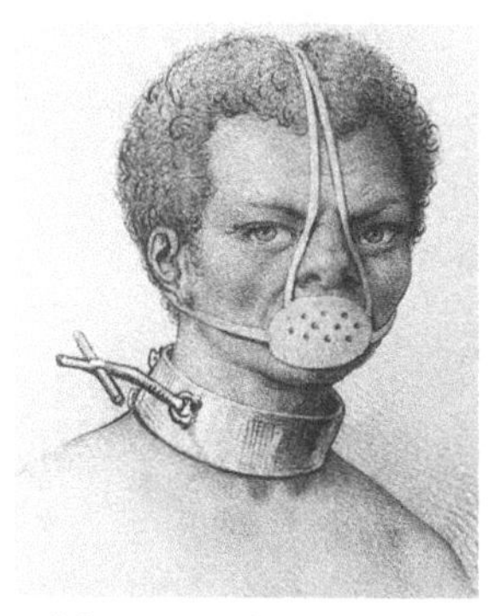

"Chatiment des Esclaves" (Brésil) 1838–1842

Once we have seen it, the image of the enslaved rebel condemned to wearing an iron collar and gag until her death never leaves us. Nonetheless, we are in fact the ones being glared upon by her eyes, which keep us fixed, seized by the inscrutable yet inescapable rebuke of her gaze. The image of the gagged Anastácia packs a punch, transferring her martyrdom to our flesh. Her story, however, is uncertain, like all the stories of enslaved Africans and their descendants. We will never have proof of what really happened with her. She was unable to express herself, her mouth permanently covered by the iron muzzle.

Oh, if only Anastácia could have spoken!

Yolanda Arroyo Pizarro manages to restore and recreate her voice, however, through the stories of Wanwe, Ndizi, Tshanwe, and Petra. No one will ever tell us who Anastácia was. It will never be those who produce a history that is imposed and considered universal who shall explain how we, Black women, truly are. It will never be those who describe us as monstrous, criminal, consumed by fury, lasciviousness, or immorality; those who define our presumed otherness. Only *we* can relate our stories. Thus, it is necessary to listen to the voices of Black women: all the pain and rage and fear, as well as the final peace. Peace that fights. Peace that rebels. Peace that gives birth to new worlds.

Notes

1 Wynter, Sylvia, "Afterword: Beyond Miranda's Meanings: Un/silencing the 'Demonic Ground' of Caliban's 'Woman.'" Boyce Davies, Carole and Elaine Savory Fido (eds.) *Out of the Kumbla: Caribbean Women and Literature*. Trenton: Africa World Press, 1990. 355-70.

2 Fuentes, Marisa J. *Dispossessed Lives: Enslaved Women, Violence, and the Archive*, Philadelphia: University of Pennsylvania Press, 2016. 5.

3 Hartman, Saidiya. *Lose Your Mother: A Journey Along the Atlantic Slave Route*, New York, Farrar, Straus & Giroux, 2007, 40.

4 Ibid., 33.

5 Brand, Dionne. *A Map to the Door of No Return. Notes to Belonging*. Toronto, Vintage Canada, 2001, 62.

6 Ibid., 48.

7 Hartman, 87.

Foreword to the First Edition

DR. MARIE RAMOS ROSADO

THE TITLE of this book suggests the theme of diversity, the question of gender and race. *Negras* comprises three narrative texts: "Wanwe," "Midwives," and "Arrowhead." The dedications and epigraphs reveal the author's intentions. She dedicates the book "to the historians," and immediately includes a quote from Guillermo A. Baralt's work, *Esclavos rebeldes. Conspiraciones y sublevaciones de esclavos en Puerto Rico*. This citation highlights the importance of slave uprisings in nineteenth-century Puerto Rico and the existing disinformation in the official record regarding slave rebellions. The movements' secretive and clandestine nature leads us to believe that the historical record is incomplete. Why did this happen? It is incomplete because historians have focused their research on rebellions led by Black enslaved men, obscuring any active participation by Black women. Puerto Rican history, like world history, has been narrated from a patriarchal perspective.

The dedication, then, is a condemnation of official history, "for leaving us out." Arroyo Pizarro is calling for the historical visibility of enslaved women. It seems that the author aims, through her fiction, to make all Black women visible and to bring to light their contributions to humankind, since Black women still seem to remain unacknowledged. She achieves her goal in this trilogy, "Wanwe," "Midwives," and "Arrowhead."

With these stories, Yolanda Arroyo Pizarro stresses the bravery and strength of Black women who "took part in thousands of individual and group escapes during slavery and post-slavery periods" (Sonya). Her narrations point to the leading roles they played in most revolts and insurrections, yet these Black women remain stricken from the official and canonical record.

This book is an homage to the work and sacrifice of all Black enslaved women in the Americas: midwives, nursemaids, witch doctors, herbalists, cross-signers, storytellers, maids, cooks, milkmaids, bone healers, etc. Furthermore, Arroyo Pizarro highlights the resistance struggles of these Black heroines by making them the main characters in each story.

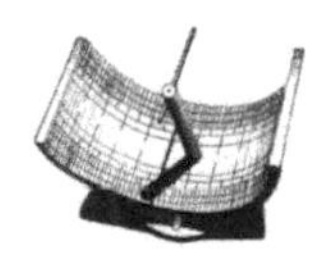

Negras &
I, Makandal

To the historians, for leaving us out.

Here we are again. . .
bodies present, color in full force,
defying invisibility,
refusing to be erased.

To Aurora, great black maroon woman of my blood,
for birthing herself from my own body.

To Zulma, my white Negra,
for her public and private displays of affection.

To my brave female predecessors:
Cocho Orta, Marie Ramos,
Mayra Santos Febres, Zaira Rivera Casellas,
Ana Irma Rivera Lassen, Ada Verdejo,
Doris Quiñones, Beatriz Berrocal,
Carmen Colón Pellot, Julia de Burgos.

To the fierce and admirable male warriors:
Roberto Ramos Perea and Daniel Luna.

Negras

Stories

Until very recently, only a limited number of nineteenth-century slave conspiracies and rebellions had been confirmed. The present research, however, mainly based on historical documents from several municipalities in Puerto Rico, shows that, contrary to what has always been believed, slaves on the island did rebel frequently. The number of known conspiracies to overtake towns or even the entire island, and attempts to kill whites, particularly overseers, adds up to more than forty. Furthermore, if we consider the secret, clandestine nature of these movements, the real number is undoubtedly higher.

—Guillermo A. Baralt, *Esclavos rebeldes: Conspiraciones y sublevaciones de esclavos en Puerto Rico* (1795–1873) (*Rebel Slaves: Slave Conspiracies and Rebellions in Puerto Rico*), Ediciones Huracán, 1982.

Black women took part in thousands of individual and group escapes during slavery and post-slavery periods on this side of the globe. They actively played central roles in most of the insurrections and revolts that were carried out, a pure manifestation of their rebelliousness. Tired as they were of the institution of slavery and all other constraints to their freedom, they transgressed, infringed, and broke with the social order.

—Gabriela Sonya

I have met brave women who are exploring the outer edge of human possibility, with no history to guide them, and with a courage to make themselves vulnerable that I find moving beyond words.

—Gloria Steinem

I get angry about things, then go on and work.

—Toni Morrison

Wanwe

1.

Her first memory might be the ship. A giant belly made of pieces of timber, joined and floating, which her people called *owba cocoo*. Such enormity, so much space. An agglomeration of logs pressed against each other; beams and planks cut and put together by some unknown procedure. Wide, embossed, ugly-colored wooden masts. Some, the ones closer to the water, are covered in moss. Wanwe has never seen them until that moment.

She is taken to the ship on a small canoe, along with other women. Their hands and legs are bound.

One of the women has stretched earlobes and a nose ring. She is not of Wanwe's clan; she doesn't even speak the same language. Unnoticed, silently, shrewdly, she unties the ropes binding her hands and legs, and suddenly jumps out of the canoe. Two men jump in the water in pursuit. They catch her, grab her torso, and beat her. The splashing water attests to the violent beating. Wanwe notices that the ocean's white foam sometimes turns red. They throw the woman back into the canoe and tie her by the neck this time. Her hands are immobilized behind her back. They pull her hair and rip out both earrings. They wait for her crying to stop and rip out her nose ring, breaking her nasal septum. Wanwe and the other women looking on understand little, but they know they are witnessing an act of control. The men tighten the shackles on the fugitive's neck, and the woman coughs and kicks.

The other women shriek. Wanwe closes her weeping eyes while the other captors move menacingly as if to strike them, a series of threatening, clumsy gestures intended to silence them. They brandish knives; they contort their eyebrows and sallow cheeks into evil expressions, flicking their tongues in and out as they shout. Their mouths reek of some type of excrement mixed with alcohol.

The veins in the neck of the woman who tried to escape bulge, they seem about to explode, and then she drools. The men keep squeezing until she faints, or until her spirit joins the powerful dancers at the gates of the afterworld. Wanwe would like to ensure her passage to the ancestral realm; she would like to say a prayer that would illuminate the embodied soul as it reaches ethereal form.

She would like to paint the forehead of the other woman, to scar her shoulders with an iron. To mark this sister in her voyage. But she can't. She is unable to act on behalf of her soul.

One of the men pulls the rope at the other end and displays the captive in front of everyone, as a lesson to the others.

2.

Prior to this moment, Wanwe has only seen the ocean twice.

The shore is a seven-day walk from her home. One must cross the entire region, sleeping out in the open, shoulder to shoulder with the other girls who do not bleed yet, and dance the *ureoré* ceremony. When she arrives at the faraway village where the ocean is visible, the elder women, as a welcoming gift, teach her how to concoct their secret war potions.

Wanwe closes her eyes and remembers the smell of the old women, her mother, her sisters, of the girls at the *ureoré* ceremony—anything that can make her forget that, at this very moment, the woman whose rings have been torn off is barely breathing.

3.

They load her onto the large ship, Wanwe and the others. Walking on deck, she sees high beams with enormous hanging cloths and moorings, of a very different material than the one used in her village. Dull, cream-colored bars, with knots in different parts of the same rope, which seem to hang in midair. The ground is hard, with splinters that sometimes pierce their heels and toes. And the stench: a foul odor reeks everywhere.

Wanwe looks at her bound hands as if noticing for the first time that defenseless extremities spring from her body, but the truth is that she has been observing herself for hours. She feels strange, as if she were outside her own flesh. She observes the events unfolding, still without fully understanding.

She presumes that the two women walking on deck in single file in front of her must be experiencing the same sensation. She even visualizes the three women behind her mulling over the same situation. She can see very little from that angle. She doesn't know how many of them are there, but she knows that they are all women.

Somehow, during the journey from her village to the beach, she has been injured in her right eye. It is oozing and hurts a great deal. She notices that there are rails from which one can gaze with longing at the coast, smell the ocean, and taste the splashing waves.

4.

The coast grows smaller as time passes, more distant. The woman walking in front of her, bearing a mark on her forehead, is still gravely ill. The mark identifies her as a member of a tribe from the south. She vomits every two or three steps, and the others struggle to keep her going. Despite their dire situation, some of the women start to sing a solemn song. Others barely let a repetitive murmur escape their parted lips, like the ones taught for morning prayer and funeral laments. When a chief or a mother of the land dies—they are given this epithet because they bear many children—their family and friends gather at the head of their deathbed and wail in mourning. Some take on the task of placing the body facedown and covering it with a blanket. They then take to the streets holding tree branches to spread the news publicly through funeral hymns. They sing in coral chants, with great pain: *epá, baba wo loni. iya li a nwa ko ri, mo de oja, ko si loja, mo de ita, ko si ni ita, mo de ile, ko si ni ile, ngko ni ri o, o da gbere, o di arinako.*

Wanwe wished she could climb a tree, grab on to a large branch, and shake it to mark the passing of the suffocated woman and her body, detached or on the verge of detachment. She can't, and senses that, from now on, she will never do so again.

5.

Her first memory could also be her village. Young boys and girls running about, playing the shoulder game.

In the *ureoré* ceremony, girls who grew up together, like sisters, sleep very close to one another, forming a line that connects them by their shoulders. After finding pastures where the grass grows over their heads, when the grownups aren't looking, the girls play *ureoré* with the boys. If the grownups caught them, they would all be punished, because the shoulder game is for girls—forbidden to boys.

First, the girls place the boys next to them, standing right beside them, and come close, arm to arm. Usually, a girl stands next to the boy she likes. Her closeness reveals which of the boys smells nice, how soft his skin is when they touch, how their heartbeats become one, because both feel it like a drumming in their chest.

Clandestine *ureoré* games take place not only hidden from the adults, but also from the smaller children, who may indiscreetly tell the grownups. It is well known that brushing shoulders is a serious prelude to the marriage ritual. Only girls who have been betrothed may touch in this manner with their chosen boys.

In Wanwe's tribe, the girl chooses the boy that she will marry. Her mother helps her choose and offers advice. Her father prepares the engagement festivities along with the chosen boy's parents. A mother may tell her daughter to pay attention to the boy's eyes, or his thick lips, his large nose, or strong arms. Those who can swim, hunt, and play the drums with great skill will come highly recommended. A girl who has bled for the first time has until her twenty-ninth cycle to choose.

6.

Wanwe remembers the engagement day of her sister, Bosuá. A boar was sacrificed, and everyone ate and drank during the ceremony. Wheat spikes from her homeland, Namib, come to mind, as well as its sand dunes, which served as a hiding place for her and her relatives while playing village games. She remembers the clicking of tongues, so particular to her regional language. She remembers, with a certain longing, how her tribe celebrates the arrival of newborns by preparing sweets from the fruit of palm trees. She remembers her sisters' long legs. How they raised and lowered them, knees bent, limbs stretched, shrieking in a trance, while dancing.

Wanwe cannot forget Bosuá's happy face, how the betrothed couple looked at each other, or how they joined their shoulders together, making their skin tremble. Wanwe and Bosuá shared a secret nobody else knew—together they had already chosen young Semö when they were all much younger. They had played that forbidden game often.

7.

The problem itself is not the game, or the closeness of the shoulders. Wanwe knows the real dilemma is the closeness of the temples and the ears. . . because sometimes, if the legs appear nervous—foot soles stumbling, knees bending, calves giving in to closeness—the shuddering in their bellies, smeared with river mud, is so powerful that sometimes the girls agree to rub brow to brow with the boys, one lip with the other.

8.

It is also possible that her first memory is the day of the kidnapping.

No one knew they would be caught.

Several mothers come out to hunt, unsuspicious, carrying their children on their backs. The only thing they need is a strong piece of fabric and a lot of hunger. In one simple movement of the cloth, the mother leans forward, places the baby over her spine, and holds the child against her body by wrapping a cloth around her and the child, and tying it with a knot. Older brothers and sisters, those who can walk, carry knives and axes with them, placed safely in their bags. They wait for the mothers to whistle, an unmistakable sign that prey approaches. If it's a short, brief whistle, the sighted animal is small. The rest of the children become excited; they know they can participate in the hunt. If it's a long, sustained whistle, the children run away and hide, but not without first handing over their weapons to their respective mothers.

Wanwe remembers seeing the tiny arms of newborns also wrapped with the strip of cloth, although the older babies like to have their arms free. A child almost never falls when the mother ties him or her to her back and goes hunting with the rest of her children. Sometimes the children cry because they don't want to be there, or they become frightened because the animal is too ferocious and makes intimidating noises. But the mother secures the child's arms by pressing them under her own; she sings a soothing song and, with assertive and experienced movements, leaves the prey lifeless within minutes.

That afternoon, despite the rain and the floods, mothers from the village paint their faces yellow and hunt enough food for several days. Some use spears to catch fish that the high water has brought within reach.

They are about to return when Wanwe and Bosuá's mother stops, warning them. She and the other mothers sense the presence of another animal, possibly large and dangerous. The animal, perhaps several, seem fearless, because instead of moving away, they come closer. The heavy rain makes it hard to discern the sounds of the approaching threat.

Wanwe and Bosuá start running at the sound of their mother's long whistle. It extends like a vine from an enormous tree—interminable. Like a fern adorned with rhizomic moss, it has no beginning or end.

Other children run now, along with their mothers; gusts of rain and darts fill the forest, missing them, piercing the skin of some. Lightning strikes, as do the forcefully thrown spears and the clubs that now hit the backs and skulls of those trying to escape.

The sound of her mother's voice, now far off, stretches out; it fades and melts into other sounds—the warnings, the dangers, the pain, the blood, the fallen bodies. Bruised bodies. Shackled hands.

Prey caught for dinner falls to the ground, rolls over the grass, through bushes with trunks and no branches, swept away by the torrential rain. The dead animals are not part of the booty. They are no longer dinner; they are now just abandoned carrion that will surely be devoured by some other beast.

9.

Wanwe is grabbed by her foot. She trips and falls. She can't see her sister; she doesn't know what happened to her. She has lost sight of her whistling mother and other siblings.

During the long seconds in which her face travels from the distance familiar to her swift feet to the one that allows gravity to knock her down, hit her head on the ground and cut her eye, she never, not for a moment, stops hearing the whistle. She turns her head, searching. Searching for her. The whistle keeps going, warning, alerting the others to the impending calamity, then is suddenly cut silent by the certain need to flee. Run far away. Get away from the enemy.

But it doesn't happen.

A curse has been brought down on them. Shouts coming from other throats. Orders to catch, to cage, take to ships, and trade their lives with the visitors from the coast.

10.

By the time Wanwe thinks again about her mother, the shoulder game, Bosuá and her young boyfriend, her siblings, *burkea* vines, *ceiba* tree roots, boars and baboons, the neighbors from the eastern empire have already tied her up and are transporting her to the shore. A shore Wanwe has seen only twice before. The journey from her home to the sea takes seven days. They have to cross a vast region, make out the coast's uniform relief, find the beach formed by large sand dunes, and sleep out in the open.

11.

During the village chants led by the elders and chiefs, Wanwe remembers listening to old legends about how, looking at the Moon, one can easily make out a frog. A frog that does not jump, but remains static and turns, the same way the eternal sphere accompanies the planet.

Mothers of the land tell their children that the frog is a lunar animal, bearer of rain, storms, and tears. It witnesses acts of injustice, especially those committed among clan brothers and sisters.

Wanwe suspects the moon animal—who belongs to the universe's wet element and who shines next to the seemingly chained stars in the dark sky—is not responsible for the kidnappings. She believes that the waters of the Moon are not responsible for the woman with the marked forehead. She does not walk in front of her anymore, as they are now kept standing in line, as if waiting their turn for some unknown event, continuously vomiting sobs or sobbing vomit.

Trying to forget so much pain, Wanwe mumbles that the amphibian on the Moon has three legs, representing the lunar phases.

12.

They are laid down, very close to one another, in the ship's cellar. So close, it seems as if they were playing *ureoré*. Wanwe looks at her two shoulder partners, one to the right, another to the left. All of them breathe with the same fright and confusion.

Men enter that dark, cramped place at the heart of the ship; they have been ordered to brand all the prisoners with fire. They use hot iron letters with the initials of those who will surely be their new owners.

13.

The ancestral beings do not come to set them free. They do not appear despite being summoned by the women with all their strength. The new deities do not listen either—the ones worshiped by the captors' shamans who wear cassocks, use a cross-shaped symbol, and throw a liquid blessed with their prayers.

Orún, Olódùmare, Bàbá, Ìyá and the goddesses who are still on the Earth do not appear, nor do the verbs conjugated from the sky, nor the wise men from the sea, nor the ancestral spirits of their clan.

Olórun has disappeared.

Oníbodè has disappeared.

Ìbí, Íyé, Áti, Ikú have disappeared.

The spirit of the river rites is nowhere to be seen. There is no walk through the Gatekeeper's door, no red paint for the dance. No more birth, life, or death.

The fears of all these women, these sisters, are reduced to one question: Who will devise our possible return? Who will embrace us in Àtúnwa after we have suffered so much? When will we be free again to play *ureoré*?

14.

The captain ties the legs of the woman who tried to escape on the shore, while the women were transported in canoes. She is barely breathing. Her bleeding ears and nostrils do not allow her to scream. She writhes in pain, struggling, but cries in silence as she is lifted by her feet.

Head down, her hands also bound, several men together hurl her into the sea.

Wanwe and the others watch the scene, trying to identify who she is. Is she one of the yellow hunters from the north, or one of the blue seamstresses from the south? Maybe one of the red dancers from the west? How many children does she have? How many times has she played? Has she worn masks in wars against other empires or in village scuffles?

The scene changes. The captain now throws a woman into the sea, and this one screams in panic. Suddenly, Wanwe makes eye contact with her, *my eyes locked with hers*, just before she sinks. The sea swallows her.

Wanwe thinks that she will drown, but the short time she is under water is enough to realize that such an end is not possible for her. Instead of this fate, there will be another.

Moments later, when she is taken out of the water by her feet and lifted, like an immortalized alabaster warrior-goddess, her body is severed in half by sharks.

15.

For the first time since leaving the jungle, Wanwe hears the whistle again. An alarm siren, announcing danger. The sound coming from that mouth is unmistakable—a sustained whistle, as long as the vines of an enormous, never-ending tree. A hole that can be heard and felt. No one knows where the sound originates, or where is it going. North, south, east, west, into the sea, out of the sea, wind, breeze, bow, deck, stern. What she does know is that the soft tingling in her ear is enough of an excuse to cry out, suffocating and sobbing, her mother's name.

My home now seemed more dreary than ever. The laugh of the little slave-children sounded harsh and cruel. It was selfish to feel so about the joy of others. My brother moved about with a very grave face. I tried to comfort him, by saying, "Take courage, Willie; brighter days will come by and by."

—Harriet Ann Jacobs, *Incidents in the Life of a Slave Girl*

Midwives

1.

The man who just entered the dungeon is dressed like a monk. I think he might be a Catholic friar. He may also be a priest or a candidate, one of those so-called seminarians. White men call candidates by a name I don't remember now. There are so many words I can't remember. I hate it when I realize somctimes that I have completely forgotten, for instance, what a giraffe is called. When I panic about all things I've forgotten, I do a mental recount: asking my mother for a hug, crying for food, calling my sisters, joking around with the smaller children. I remember those phrases in my language perfectly. There are others that come to mind in other tongues, depending on the time I've spent on certain plantations, surrounded by people from other clans. I also remember words in Spanish: lullabies for the masters' children, recipes learned at Spanish ports, market spices, how to prepare meat, prayers by the holiest of Christians. I even know a few words of the natives' language, the ones the white men call "Taino," who are becoming scarce. And if I concentrate hard enough, while I suffer my eleven days of penance in this dungeon, amid all this solitude, I can recite some sort of hymn sung by the Dutch, some sort of chant in which they despised a land called France.

But I am not alone anymore. The foreman and the night watchman have come into the cell with a man wearing a tunic. I once wore an outfit just like it when I tried to escape with a group of Mandingos. Black Mandingos came from the sea once while I was working by the beach, on the way to the sugar mill at Hacienda Segovia. They were Black runaways who abandoned ship before it docked. No one had seen them, or at least no one was after them yet. They covered me in a wet, spare cassock, and I joined them. They were three men and a woman, malnourished and dehydrated. I guided them so they could steal food and stayed by their side voluntarily, even though, on the fifth day, they had lain with me without my consent. The woman looked away, trembling. Then they lay with her as well. I am not Mandingo, yet a sense of loyalty kept me by their side, and I served as an interpreter, because they did not understand the masters' tongue. Although I am not *ladina*, I understand it perfectly. I understand it, but that is a deeply kept secret.

2.

The monk is white, yet different. I think I can discern a look of surprise and compassion in his pink eyes, if such a thing exists among the conquistadors. Even among priests and nuns, I never sense a hint of solidarity with us. This man is different. There is something about him.

"Do you speak Spanish?" he asks, and I stare at him that first time. I pretend not to understand, and the foreman hits me in the face, claiming that I do. He demands that I answer, but I keep silently staring at the monk. He touches his chest and says, "Petro." I do the same and answer, "Ndizi." He repeats my name, pronouncing all three syllables separately, through the nose. I nod my head in approval.

Then Petro begins a recital of regional dialects, trying his luck: Kimbundu, Mandingo, Bantu, French, Dutch, and Creoles from these languages. I tell myself, "I must be careful with this man." I must remember never to tell him everything I know, what I have seen, what I have felt. Ever. I decide to answer in the tongue of the Yoruba, and he smiles. As best he can, he tells me in that language: "I promise to practice more Yoruba, and I'll come back to talk to you in a few days." Without meaning to do so, I smile back. The foreman and the night watchman do not seem pleased.

A while later, Petro says goodbye, and leaves. I watch him as he exits my cell. He passes through the door to the outside, to freedom, a place that is no longer mine. It was once. Once, in my native village, where I played with herds of zebra and with my grandmothers; I had several grandmothers, and they taught me how to make potions. When I think of freedom, I think of all the words for it in all the languages I know in which this means something. And the same thing happens when I think of the word "laziness" or "rest"—I don't remember how to say them in every language I know. I also don't know the Wolof word for "whip," although I can speak the Congolese word for it. Then the foreman and the night watchman hit me again, tie me up, and penetrate me with their rancid penises.

3.

The second time Petro visited us—I say "us" because now I have company; they have incarcerated a new midwife next to me—he came with a book I thought was the Bible. I later found out it wasn't. It's a series of papers on which he has written some phrases in Yoruba. He reads them to me, and I answer. Slowly. Imitating the lack of fluency that all language learners display. He asks me my age, and I tell him that, according to the northern tribes' way of counting, I'm in my thirties. Then I explain, in broken Spanish, that I was kidnapped by the empire of the Blacks from the coast and sold to the whites over fifteen years ago. For more than a decade,

I was forced to work as a cook, a cane worker, and a midwife. "What do you cook?" he asks in the Christian tongue; I counter, speaking the slave language now, with the first thing that comes to mind—something about cooking headless pigs and sweetbread, tails and ears of animals. I tell him anything, with few details; the truth is I can cook whatever you put in from of me, and quite well, by the way. I can even prepare slow-acting poison, seasoned with *guarapo*, a sugar-based alcoholic drink, and cinnamon.

Petro pronounces Yoruba phonemes, some fluid, some broken. He constructs a phrase with a conjunction that seems to be "*mtoto*": *m.'to.to / niño / petit nené*, or something like that. I nod, and he stares at me for a long while. He wants to know if the charges against me are true.

The midwife next to me cries, and he is confused. He thinks she is mourning the dead children.

4.

I remember, half awake, half asleep, the bonfires during my escape with the Yoruba. We light pyres with pieces of wood and palm trees because it's cold and too dark at night. We manage to find some caves and hide there until we are sure we have lost our pursuers. There we light torches, rest, and outline a plan for our return to the continent. After hours of discussion, we give up. It will never happen. We would need resources—barges, weapons, supplies for the return trip, and other necessities we do not have. We decide that dying would be better than bowing before the oppressor, and we talk about some of our brothers who were experts in compassionate suicide; they had done it, and had left instructions as their legacy. I mentioned Undraá, who was forced to cohabit with the white men on the ship that took us from the continent to the island, a woman who knows the sea and its species for she lived among the yellow fisherwomen for many years. She waited until the ship reached the open sea, near the sharks' nests. Then she jumped into the water. The Yoruba mention other brothers. Bguiano, an expert tusk hunter from the Sahara region, a member of an army of men who would continually sharpen their teeth and kill jungle beasts by fighting with their bare hands and biting. He put together a group of newcomers at the plantation where he served, and taught them his skill. Then, they all made an oath before Ṣàngó, and would rip off with a single bite the most visible, beating vein in the neck of those who wished them to. We remember Zeza, a potion brewer and spell caster, who knew the right combination of every poisonous herb in the region for closing one's eyes and never opening them again. And so we go on, bringing up ideas one by one, while some doze off.

I yawn and make an oath to the gods of the wind, whose existence I already doubt—If I am ever caught again, the children shall pay.

5.

Petro gently taps my face, to wake me up. I drink in his pink, familiar gaze. He pours water and medicine made from pain-killing herbs down my throat to ease the pain in my body. "You were talking in your sleep," he says, and when the jailer passes nearby, he makes as if he were praying with his rosary in Latin. He then cobbles together syllables from different languages to explain to me that I am not an animal. *Mbwa / 'm.bwa / dog; tembo / elefant / thembo / elefante; ne.nda / not / no; you / toi*. There is a rebellious empathy in his voice that makes me believe him, and even feel sorry for him. I mumble in French, and he freezes, surprised at my proficiency in the language. I repeat the phrase in Spanish and Igbo. Petro covers my mouth with his hand, so that I'll be silent and not be found out. The guards are coming. They feed the other two women in my cell leftovers from the neighboring plantations, but nothing for me. I've been declared a Seditious and Subversive Black Woman by the public bulletins—identified by the birthmark near my eye, the P-shaped mark branded on my forehead—and a reward is offered for my capture. When they leave, Petro takes out some casaba he had concealed, and puts it in my mouth, inviting me to chew it slowly, so that I do not choke. The other women share their water with me. Everything tastes like the candy they make in the valley near our native river during the ceremony of masks.

With a clicking like the tribal musical laments played when my people are captured, fricative and guttural sounds, aspirated possessives, stuttering, short consonants, long vowels, and other grammatical curiosities, Petro assures me that he will keep my secret. All he wants is to know, to document this violence, this inhumanity, that has been unleashed in our world, he explains, all this historical bestiality. There are friars on other islands writing chronicles about these things; I want to tell your story. We act as friends to the crown, but it is not so. I swear I won't bring you any trouble.

"Do you swear on your god?" I warn him, and when he says that he does, I rebuke him: "Your god has no power or strength; he is lazy, weak, useless. How can he allow this to happen?" Petro nods. He lowers his head in what I can only interpret as an act of shame. He asks me who are my gods, if I believe in Babalú-Ayé, Oiá, Obàtálá. . . I tell him, "I believe in none of them," and tears spring from my eyes. "They all abandoned us."

6.

I swear that I would rather die, Fray Petro, than be used as an animal. I swear that I wanted to kill them all, my dear father. *Nous allons reproduire une armeé, kite a kwanza yon lame*. That is what I set out to do. That is what we women set out to do, and we spread the word through the beating of our drums.

Hebu kuzaliana jeshi. We repeated it at music gatherings to the Wolof, Touareg, Bakongo, Malimbo, and Egba. The news continued to spread in chant to the Balimbe, Ovimbundu, and the rest. Those of us from Congo, those of us from Ibibio, and those of us from Seke or Cabinda, all of us women responded. *Hagámonos un ejército*. Let us breed an army.

The problem of those who oppress, Fray Petro, is not oppression itself, but rather the underestimation of the oppressed. I always pay attention to the expressions of vitality or exhaustion on the faces of those who enter the body of a woman without her permission. In my village, if something like that were to happen, the transgressors would be punished and fined according to what they owned. If a man raped a woman, whether young or old, single or married, he would have to pay with his possessions. And if he did not have any, he would pay by chopping off, in cold blood, any appendage—an arm, a hand, a foot, an ear, even the nose. We women were encouraged to defend ourselves, to hit back, bite, and tear. Things have changed since Blacks started kidnapping other Blacks and selling us to the Portuguese or other whites, to ship us away. Now we are encouraged not to defend ourselves because we belong to a master. Oppressors have such liberties, yet they underestimate us.

I always pay attention to the expressions of vitality or exhaustion on the faces of those who enter the body of a woman without her permission, Fray Petro. And so, I came upon a face overcome with ecstasy one afternoon, an unknown night watchman, just after forcing himself upon me. He didn't even care that Oshun's blood was running down my thighs on one of my lunar days. He closed his eyes for a second, exhausted. It only took a second to realize that he was alone. . . that it was going to be easy for me. He tilted his head back, as if engulfed by the pleasure of his ejaculation, and became distracted. I bit him. I took my teeth up to his glans and I closed them, rabidly, like a mad dog. At first, he tried to hit me. But then at once he fell, disoriented and wounded, in great pain. While he grabbed himself, unbalanced and moaning on the floor, I took the keys from his pants, unbolted the cage, locked it behind me, and stopped at each cell, one by one. I freed ladinos, runaways, and native slaves. And the midwives, my sisters in battle.

7.

Witch doctor, herbalist, bone healer, midwife. I have embodied every task of a domestic slave to gain access to white newborns. Following the instructions of a great Black witch, stationed at a hacienda belonging to Dominican cathedral Porta Coeli, I have blessed them with the sign of the cross and treated them for bellyaches. I smear my hands with concoctions and place anesthetic herbs on their gums when they are teething. I've had them suck on my breast until milk comes out to become their nursemaid. I invent stories for them; I untangle their hair with silver combs; I fluff skirts for rich girls and pants for the little masters. I cook for them and prepare their teas. I milk the udders from their favorite cows and goats to feed them once they crawl or begin to walk.

I gain their trust gradually. We all do the same, and we are many; we gain their trust gradually. Then I start helping to bring the children of African-born Black slave women into the world. They are the hardest Black women to tame, say the whites. In truth, I am one of them, but I behave like a *ladina*. I speak Spanish and wear skirts and petticoats even when I work in the fields; I kneel at the right moment during mass and at processions for imaginary Catholic virgins. No one knows I speak the Hausa's tongue, or the Fulani's, or that I stand behind the walls and listen to the pronunciation of my masters and his visitors from the militia, and later practice it when I'm alone.

On the twentieth day of my fifth imprisonment, I am taken out of my cell to undergo the corporal punishment prescribed by my sentence. The plantation's book lists all my offenses: disobedience, defiant behavior, insolence, excessive idleness, inciting rebellion, and, finally, escaping. And now this, the worst crime of all. A mestizo woman, whom I recognize from the last birth I carried out, ties my hands behind my back. She pushes me. She spits on me. The executioner says that I belong to an animal race, soulless and heartless. A priest recites the prayers of the rosary, which they have taught us so selflessly at our masters' homes. He orders me in Spanish to repeat after him. At first, I don't comply, until the lashing begins.

I remember the village shaman chanting, trying to summon protection from pain. I imagine that reciting The Lord's Prayer and Hail Mary repeatedly can do the same. In a final attempt at resistance, I manage to untie my legs and crawl, hands bound. The guards stop me and hit me even harder, then ask permission to repeat the flagellation. But a high official will not let them, and they stop. They don't hit me anymore.

On the way back to the dungeon, I recognize Petro, walking beside me. He extends his hand to me, and I give him mine. I hear I've been sentenced to death by hanging. I faint.

8.

At my request, Petro describes the last three sunsets he has seen from some balcony in the walled city. *L'orange, la vanille, roze*. Pink, above all. I tell him that in my village children who are born like him, and with his eye color, are worshipped; people offer them and their parents presents until they accumulate a small fortune. Once they grow up, the bravest warriors take care of their courtship, and marry them to the most deserving. The warriors' first and second wives assist in the election.

On the day my sentence is to be carried out, someone comes to shave my head. Petro asks permission from his monastery to perform the last rites. But I am not baptized, and the matter ends there. They at least allow him to join the procession escorting me to the gallows where the noose awaits. Petro notices that I remain unperturbed; he holds my face in his hands and repeats the confession ritual. "O Mary." "Conceived without sin," I answer. "Tell me your sins, child." I close my eyes, but there are no tears. "I have none!" I reply. Petro hugs me, improvises some sort of ritual with the sign of the cross, and tries to keep me on my feet. Everyone is watching us—lieutenants, sea captains, plantation owners and their wives, adolescents and children set to inherit a hacienda, a dozen Black midwives accused for the first or second time and the officers who escort them, hoping my sentence may be a lesson to these women. A white nursemaid, who nurses white babies, shaves my head in front of everyone. Owners who had lost merchandise on my account applaud.

"Ndizi, what did you do to them? I need this and other atrocities to be known." "It's my secret under seal of confession, my dear father," I tell him, "Forgive me." And he insists, "What must I forgive?"

Silence.

And a revelation. In a low voice, in our dialect—Fray Petro's and mine—I tell him, "I drown the babies in the placenta bucket, my dear father. I press my hands into their little black throats, and suffocate them. Or I asphyxiate them with their own umbilical cords, sometimes even before they come out of the womb. The mothers don't notice it, or they want it, or have asked for it. . . begged for it in a tongue unknown to the whites. The act, which can be quite subtle, seems normal to the newborn keeper, who is meant to secure the survival of the future slave. I outwit him. We all outwit him. If I can't do it at birth, I later feed them fruit tainted with the blood of women infected with tetanus from their chains. Or I collect diarrhea from dysentery outbreaks and mix it with their purées. I sometimes smear my nipple with the concoction and then nurse them. Or I put dry casaba close to their tonsils and block their breathing. I am not the only one. Many follow me. We have bred an army."

More silence.

I take a mental inventory of forgotten words. I repeat their sound. I articulate by touching the back of my tongue with the back of my soft palate. Suddenly there is a narrowness in my air passages. Air does not pass. I feel my uvula amid a strong radiance. I am all vibratory contractions. I am a choking pharynx—moon, energy, courage, eternity.

The last thing I see are his pink eyes.

Even the smallest victory is never to be taken for granted. Each victory must be applauded.

—Audre Lorde

Arrowhead

1.

The master walks hesitantly around the two female slaves. He unties his boots, one by one, and seems to stop his gait by looking at the shadows on the walls. He does not do it; he does not stop. He unties his knickers by releasing the suspenders at the neck, and continues circling the room, illuminated only by candlelight. Later, earnestly, he finally touches Tshanwe's fleshy breasts, and she lowers her gaze. He calls her Teresa, but she doesn't know why.

Tshanwe's nappy black hair does not fall over her face, and the blouse her master lifts is not made from imported linen. Despite this, he seems to enjoy the difference of a firmer, younger flesh, which his wife no longer possesses, but Tshanwe does, under her dark skin. The countess has given birth to seven of his descendants, and now she simply devotes her days to the craft of mundillo lacemaking. Such effortless activity, practiced in the bedchambers, has not suited her body well, due to lack of exercise. Her permanent stay at the colonial residence has turned her pale and softened her muscles. When she moves her extremities to draw the curtains in the main room, the fluffy flesh on her forearms overflows, trembling all over, just like the sweets that Jwaabi, a slave, cooks over a fire. The desserts tremble and wiggle as much in the pot as they do in the jar. The slave prepares them according to instructions from the count himself, who in turn called for local sweets strictly made from a book of indigenous recipes, a gift one of his friends had brought from the capital.

The master removes Tshanwe's mud-stained skirt and spreads her legs with one hand. He calls her Teresa again. He touches her pubis and studies it with hungry eyes. Some of his fingers are also caught in awe. He pushes the Black woman to the bed, not before drawing the mosquito net. Then he comes in and out; in and out of her.

The other slave, Jwaabi, remains standing, in the middle of the room, hands behind her back. She shamelessly awaits her turn.

2.

The morning in which little master Gregorio's dog died, Tshanwe was helping Jwaabi peel vegetables. She did not fully understand the situation. Tshanwe was Count Georgino

Pizarro's last acquisition from the slave market at the capital, and for this reason, she did not speak the masters' language at all. She did not understand the code of the natives either, the ones they called Taino, whose language was so essential for cooking. She had been separated from her family in her homeland and had barely survived the trip across the ocean. She understood Jwaabi's tongue even less, nor the language of the servants in charge of Hacienda Pizarro, because almost all of them came from different ethnic groups, spread throughout the large continent.

Tshanwe understood only a few words in Spanish, even when they were pronounced slowly—*ven* (come here), *comida* (food), *castigo* (punishment). On the other hand, she did recognize the name the masters used to called Jwaabi. Every time the mistress yelled "Juana," Tshanwe would see Jwaabi run to her side and help her with one of the children, or assist her with the bucket. The countess had a phobia of excrement, and the mere idea of touching it seemed to upset her stomach. For this reason, she didn't even wipe her own ass. She would yell, "Juana," after doing her business, and the slave then would run over to her and clean her up, and later take away the feces in the washbowl. Tshanwe assumed that "Jwaabi" and "Juana" were the same person.

On that morning, while preparing the meal, Tshanwe heard little master Gregorio speaking loudly from the living room. He was speaking between sobs. He insisted on repeating the phrase, "He's dead, and no one knows why." He cried deeply, with a crying that struck the newcomer, who was still taking everything in, as excessive; children in her village had never cried that way, except on the day of the loud explosions. Tshanwe examined the boy from afar, behind the curtain, showing herself a little. She observed the dog, breathless on the wooden floor. She looked at master Georgino and assumed he was scolding the boy. He spoke with a loud voice and mentioned the dead again. The little master repeated, "I don't know." Tshanwe went away to the kitchen, and before she resumed her kitchen duties, peeling vegetables, as the other Black woman instructed her with a gesture, she made a face.

"Dead?"

Jwaabi nodded without raising her eyes from the meat she was cutting. Tshanwe stared at her as if to ask a question, making sure she was looking at her this time.

"Dead?"

Jwaabi spoke in her dialect. She shrugged her shoulders. Given that she still had a doubtful face, she opened her hands and waved them.

"No one knows why," she replied.

3.

Tshanwe was chosen one afternoon to carry all the crossbows—the owner's and his guests'—to the place where the men practiced their gallantry. It was a steep but even meadow that extended out of sight, beyond the hacienda, somewhat farther than the cane scrublands. At first, the load seemed unbearable, but she got used to the weight and was able to make it there. Once the shooting began, targeting the wide grove, Tshanwe stood still, contemplating the silence of the sky. The morning of the dog's death came to her mind.

That morning, she waited for two slaves to move the lifeless animal to the stables. They laid it on the table, waiting to dig a hole in the ground for its burial. Under the count's orders, the Black men headed to the place where dead animals and slaves are buried. While they were digging, she walked up to the animal and touched it. She noticed blood on one of its sides and, examining its fur, found a hole in the skin. The wound was not too deep; she touched the end of it with her index finger. She discovered an object embedded in the skin. Not stopping until she satisfied her curiosity, she manipulated the carcass with her nails until she extracted the piece. It was an arrowhead.

Tshanwe kept it as an amulet.

She wondered if this was what was meant by the phrase pronounced "no-one-knows-why." She did know that similar phrases, like "I don't know," "no one knows," or "I don't know why," meant something related to ignorance. She reached that conclusion because everyone would shrug their shoulders.

4.

On the morning of the counts' wedding anniversary, the count left very early, at daybreak, to practice with the bow. But he would do something else first. He came into the slaves' room and woke up Tshanwe and the cook. He took them up to the shed. On that occasion, while whispering the name "Juana," he penetrated Jwaabi first, leaving the other slave to watch. Then he mounted Tshanwe, calling her "Teresa." Once finished, he took Tshanwe by the arm and dragged her to the weapons room. He put the arrow bags in one of her arms and one of his two crossbows in the other. Then he walked in front of her, guiding her to the slope.

Maybe the hour betrayed him—it was too early—but the count soon grew tired and returned to the hacienda. Maybe it was the drink that betrayed him, the one he swallowed in such quantities, straight from the leather canteen he almost always carried with him. He left Tshanwe alone, surrounded by butterflies and grasshoppers, by the greenery adorned with hues of blue, typical of the morning light. Tshanwe let herself fall to the earth, exhausted. She slept on the morning dew that covered the grass just for few moments. But then she immediately rose to her feet. Before she decided to put the heavy bags on her shoulders to go back, she took an arrow, and loaded a bow. She mumbled, "no one knows why," and shot the arrow into the distance, towards the trees.

5.

The count's festivities ended in disaster when Trino, the master's eldest son, tried—and failed—to wrestle his father, just before sunset. They started by throwing punches into the air, amid an excess of alcohol and laughter. Then they moved over to hold each other's heads and sides, trying to trip one another, gripping firmly, almost to the extent of asphyxiation. Suddenly, one of them pushed hard, and the young man's knuckles struck the older man's jaw.

The ruckus was heard beyond the limits of the hacienda. Count Georgino, accustomed to a more gentlemanly restraint, broke and let out a loud cry, followed by several moans, like a mule.

While the countess intervened by using a cloth that Tshanwe had brought to stop the count's profuse bleeding, his hunting mates came to his aid, preventing him, as dizzy as he was, from falling. Tshanwe remained there, puzzled, staring at the shiny blood, its wetness, its consistency, its thickness, so like other bloods. The fluid gushed from the white man almost in the same way as it flowed from the men and women of her native Namaqua.

6.

That night, while sleeping on the piece of earth that sometimes served as a bed, Tshanwe played with the idea of returning to her people one day, of seeing them grow old among the wisemen and their magic, of touching their faces tattooed with pigments of plants from across the desert. The memory of that desert came to mind, the one in Namib, the one with the sand dunes where she and her relatives hid while playing in the village. She remembered the distinctive clicking sound of her native tongue, and how Namaqua celebrated the birth of a child with sweets made from the fruit of the palm tree. She turned over and touched the tip of her new amulet. She caressed it with her fingertips. She whistled, and the sound melted into the night and the frogs' croaking. If someone would answer her whistle, if only someone would. . .

The feeling reminded her of the times when she heard the Namaqua women announcing a coming war. They would paint themselves under the eyes and under their noses with a paste made out of spices, with colors that resembled the dawn. They would carry a lance and their other weapons tied behind their backs. The other peoples, all over the interior plateau, would call them the yellow warriors, known for their poisoned arrows. Women with no fear. Or at least fearless until they—and their families—became prisoners of creatures with lighter skin, who came in ships and put them in chains. They would tie them up with sorcery. The spell consisted in making their flesh explode, forcing them to surrender. Sleep finally overtook Tshanwe.

7.

They had her pinned. The corner sheltered her for a while, but only for a moment, until the little masters came closer threateningly, closing in on her. They had taken her by surprise. She was on her way back from accompanying the count at the shooting range, and the marks left by the bag straps still showed on the skin of her shoulders. That afternoon, like so many others in which she had planned to get away for a while during the return from the slope, two attackers came before her. They forced her back little by little, emboldened by the weapons one of the little masters held in his left hand, the other, in his right. The bigger one, Trino, who was barely taller than her, held an instrument similar to her amulet, broken in half and sharp. As if it were a foil, he would launch it forward and back again—towards and away from

Tshanwe—with a gracious movement of the wrist. Gregorio had one of the countess' bobbing-lace needles, and he would move it around until it struck a thigh, arm, or calf of her black skin.

Tshanwe opened and closed her eyes. She tried unsuccessfully to summon guardian spirits. Once again, she dodged Trino's attack just when Gregorio made her bleed again with a jab in her armpit. She heard the boys says, "you're like a dog," "Black blood is not the same," but she couldn't understand what they were saying.

She then moves forward, trying to run, despite being hurt. But this time, Trino does not miss. She almost dodges him, but the broken arrow cuts Tshanwe's face. Gregorio seizes the opportunity to stretch out the needle and stick it in Tshanwe's open hand, right in the palm. As soon as more dark red fluid spouts, they both shout, "Real blood!"

They don't stop. They keep sticking their blades, piercing flesh without mercy. The slave's breasts, neck, and abdomen are marked with cuts like tattoos. Her new marks make the warm fluid run and make her fall on her knees, weakened.

She struggles to catch her breath, if only for a millisecond, and snatches away the sharp object from Trino's hand, even while hunched over. She dismisses—as possible consequences of defending herself—thoughts of the dungeon, the gallows, the high beam over the trap where they tie her hands and legs, and the rope stretching neck and limb, pulled by one of the master's horses. Such a stock of images clouds her reasoning for an instant, but she promptly rejects them. In her first act of self-defense, trying to persuade her attacker to leave her alone, Tshanwe brandishes the sharp object toward the taller *señorito*; the sharp object is now embedded in his middle finger. Trino cries out in pain, catching his younger brother's attention. It was a matter of time before the count appeared between the two.

The master's beating began with a shower of punches and kicks to her face. She watches him stop and yell at the boys. He hits her in the torso. "Slaves are expensive," "she's my property." Hits to the back, now. "You senseless boys!" "You'll see who's in charge, you filthy nigger!" Tshanwe does not understand and falls to the ground, powerless. She notices, sobbing, that the count is also beating the boys. She sees how his face changes when he sees one of his children wounded, his concern, his wrath. At first, she manages to crawl into a fetal position, protecting herself from a few fractures. Nonetheless, her arms and hips end up dislocated in the end. The leather canteen, now empty, rolls on the floor. Now the *señoritos* and the count's hunting mates join the scuffle. Tshanwe loses consciousness.

8.

Agile as a gazelle, free as if she were on the rocky, enormous steppe of her homeland. She runs, she flees. She smears herself in war paint, announcing a storm of darts and spears. She jumps over the bed of sandstone that extends beyond the oscillating dinosaur tracks on its surface. She walks, lethargic, through the jungle, home of the petrified enemy. She hears a clicking of the tongue, an order for mass execution. A whistling answered by more whistling. Tshanwe refuses to expire; she rejects her own death. The will of her ancestors and her courage lead her back to the tunnel. Do not fall, odalisque. Do not perish, gladiator. The time of past ages calls for you. The water transporting pinewood to this arid land, burying the logs in the mud as centuries pass, demands your existence. Thousands of zebras, antelopes, and gnus, myriads of elephants, lions, and giraffes lead the carnival of wounds, licking the rotten meat after the battle.

Rivers have turned to sand. Water currents are no more than muddy, infected holes. Thousands of cattle, goats, sheep, and camels have surrendered and fallen over the dry and broken land that no longer nurses life. Now this land has an excess of scarcity; her daughters have been snatched.

9.

Two strong Black slaves carry Tshanwe by her arms and legs; they don't understand each other either, but they are gradually learning the language of the masters. Following the count's instructions, they must burry her where the dogs and the Blacks are buried. Rain falls, so they place her over a wooden platform where no one officiates any funeral rites or ceremonies of any kind. They leave her body alone for a few hours, return to other duties, waiting for the rain to pass, and then dig a hole to place her in before her flesh begins to rot and smell.

Raindrops revive her eyelids, and an invisible shaman wakes her up. Namqua and its female warriors protect her. The body disappears. So does one of the master's crossbows. Three days later, nobody can explain such sorcery. No one understands such witchcraft. The master and his men first throw their own arrows at the lush grove, as they usually do. Another morning practicing archery. Some sort of spell, however, makes one of the arrows come back, like a boomerang. The arrow thrown from the grove at the end of the slope emits a whistling sound. The spirits answer—it's the only possible explanation. The missile drives into Count Georgino's forehead. No one knows how.

Nurslings

1.

It was hard for Petra to accept the little master's new comportment. Since he had reached what is considered legal age for a young plantation owner, his interests had been changing. When he was a pale, chubby, happy baby, smiling as soon as he felt Petra's breasts swollen with food, there was no problem at all. It was no problem either for the enslaved woman to canalize the anxiety that the little master suffered upon attending school in San Juan. On the day he was enrolled at the school led by the famous teachers by the name of Cordero, he developed a rash.

In the classroom to which little Jonás was assigned, there were other children from the landowning class, boys and girls of good white families, owners themselves of slaves, peons, and overseers. Most of them were known to the *señorito*. They had played together, trained in fencing and horseback riding, attended parties and balls on the outskirts of the town and on neighboring haciendas. Both Maestro Rafael and his sister, Celestina, also taught Black children. Some were born in Africa (the *bozales*); others were mulatto, mestizo, and even quadroons born on the island. Dark-skinned pupils were not mixed with white youths; therefore, it was promptly concluded that the illness cannot have been contracted by direct contact with such bestialized creatures as the former. Hence, the apothecary diagnosed a condition of detachment, caused by the change in environment.

The owner of Hacienda Cartagena, also Petra's owner and mistress, immediately ordered the Black *ladina* to take the little master to his daily lessons, plant herself at the doors of the inner patio of the Cordero residence, and offer her tit to the boy upon his request. Petra obeyed and was even better off for such an arrangement, because during her waiting hours, she performed no greater task than knitting wool clothes for her nursling, Jonás Cartagena. In addition, she had to be provided with food in good condition and plenty of water, so that the milk she lavished upon the cherub would be abundant and high in nutrients. The itching caused by the young man's rash disappeared in a few days.

2.

Petra was born in San Juan Bautista and is of Mandingo descent on her maternal grandmother's side, as the old woman herself told her on nights brimming with lullabies and as the little master confirmed when he asked Maestro Cordero about the origin of his slaves. With atypical obsession, and as he grew in height and age, Jonás insisted on discussing the matter of her origin on several occasions. This was how he became familiarized with a map found in the office of his deceased father, which delineates the territory between Cabo Blanco and Cabo Las Palmas, Senegal, Cape Verde, and Sierra Leone on the African continent. And this was how Celestina Cordero patiently came to explain the trade route, to quell the young man's curiosity. The boy remembers the day in which he secretly asked the small group of young white classmates. He asked about the service of Black enslaved women; he asked why some of them are held in good esteem when they should be beasts of burden, when they should be inferior. He even inquires about abolition, a topic he has heard some men talk about on the downlow while heading for the taverns. Such a compromising word—*abolitionist*. To grow up and to fight for the good of all people. To free those who are not free. To forge a better world.

He raises questions because he does not understand. But one of the boys answers, lowering his voice, "My father says that Black women are here only to be mounted. They are more enjoyable than white women". Jonás Cartagena is stunned; he will never be the same again.

3.

And so, the *señorito*'s current fixations do not necessarily revolve around sucking Petra's teats for nourishment. For some time now, the tall and strong youth of fourteen years has been taking the reins of his inherited plantation, besieging the female slave quarters at night, and sometimes even standing quietly very close to Petra's leaf cot.

She sees him, pretends to be asleep, and continues breathing as if snoring to give the impression that she is unaware of such intentions. She also realizes that the young master follows her in secret during the day, that he comes close so he can smell her while she nurses other Spanish and Creole babies, that he touches her legs for no reason, that he draws her image on pieces of paper which he hides so he can rub them all over his body when he lies by himself.

Last week, Jonás stood at a strategic place between the laundry room and some bushes. Petra felt his presence when it was too late, and the young master was rubbing back and forth the piece of meat and skin with which white men rape the women of her kind.

4.

After several days, Petra is assigned to nurse a pair of newborn twins birthed by the sister of her owner mistress, Jonás's mother. The mistress wants her nephews to grow and develop with as good a disposition and as strong a frame as the young plantation owner. On the afternoon that the twins are to be baptized, they are given to Petra so that she can nurse them both at the same time, on her lap.

After nursing the babies, Petra witnesses how they are carried along a celebratory procession toward the cathedral. All members of the Cartagena family and many plantation officers head to the sacramental ceremony that, as she was told, would be performed by the bishop himself. Everyone would return late, on the break of dawn, because there would be a feast after the rite. Everyone except Jonás, who returns two hours later, alone.

Petra is knitting two pairs of booties for the twins by candlelight in one of the rooms. Her breasts are bothering her, they rather hurt, from nursing two at the same time; her nipples receive twofold stimulation, bringing about a burst of colostrum. Milk trickles down all over her belly.

The *señorito* arrives. He opens and closes all the doors. He searches every room. He stares upon finding her. He walks near the rocking chair and, in a single movement of the hand, with his fingers, he unties the cotton blouse made solely for Black wetnurses. Petra closes her eyes, vanquished. She cannot believe the assault that renders her something different for that child.

Jonás feels her marbled breasts, of a dark jasper color. Honey-flavored Mandingo breasts, captives of a Senegalese ruler, rising before him. Skins born of some warrior empire. He has read about Petra's ancestors in *Document on Charters of the Indies and the New Colonies of 1793*. He has memorized the words. He wants to offer her this detail of human knowledge on some occasion. To sing it if he had the chance and if it were possible. To tell her; to tell her waist. Her thighs. Her blackest of breasts. Jonás kneels and puts his lips over the creamy cascade. He puts her nipples in his mouth. He presses hard and begins sucking, tears running down his cheeks, as he opens her legs.

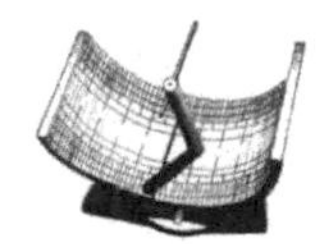

I, Makandal

Poems

To Raúl Guadalupe

To Josué Santiago

To Miguel Rodríguez López

I shall be Makandal
in the ointments of plants
that'll wage war against the veins
of the Anglo-Yankee imperialists
condemning my Brown people
to the slavery of drugs
and to Black Fridays
of foreign companies

I shall be Makandal Albizu
on the morning when bells
shall leave their brown poison tea
in the throats of our masters
in Congress or the White House
where humans are still being sold

— Raúl Guadalupe

Birth of a Poetry Book

THE JOURNEY of writing this book began when I started my doctoral studies in 2016, encouraged by people whom I love and admire—Miguel Rodríguez López, Luis López Nieves, Sandra Guzmán, Manuel Figueroa, Zulma Oliveras Vega, and Waleska Semidey. My beloved friend, the adoptive son that life itself gifted me, writer David Caleb Acevedo, had just recommended writing a diary to balance my emotions, as I faced melancholic and romantic complications back then. Thus, I engaged in reflective daily writing to seize the situation and understand myself. Eventually, Dr. Raúl Guadalupe—my professor of HILI 1012: Afro-descendent History and Literature and HILI 1009: Historical Problems and Twentieth Century Puerto Rican Literature—challenged us to write a weekly dialogical reflection for his course, and this book began to take shape inadvertently, in dribs and drabs. These writings were born as or were converted into poetic reactions that I included in Dr. Guadalupe's assignments. I also added some creative contestations sparked by another seminar, LITE 1611: Antillean Literature I: From the Myths of the Taíno to Modernism, taught by Dr. Josué Santiago. Reading one of the best books that have been written on the topic—The Gospel of Makandal and the Rainmakers, by Guadalupe himself (Editorial Tiempo Nuevo 2015)—provided the final inspirational push I needed. Political and historical events framed a very uncertain time during which my heart was split on account of romantic abyss and social disarray. One of Guadalupe's poems was one of the timeliest lessons I have received in life and serves as an epigraph for this book. I had just submitted a paper to Dr. Guadalupe regarding Alejo Carpentier's *The Kingdom of This World,* amid a vortex of conflicts triggered by the blatant and rampant racism that overwhelms Puerto Rico. A recent manifestation was a blackface trend that seemed to resurge in the media like an ancient, oppressive boomerang. Therefore, along with my paper, I handed my professor a poetic tirade titled "The Kingdom of This Mockery," which evolved into a poem called "I, Makandal." When Raúl Guadalupe returned my graded work, on the feedback he provided at the footer of the page, he had transcribed by hand the quoted answer/poem. Indeed, it was a great lesson for me. It was as if the professor were telling me: "Go on, poet. Feel. Live. Write, for poetry always prevails."

"Blessed be the day in which it shall be a woman who falls defending the freedom of her homeland. On that day, there will be a revolution in every Puerto Rican home, and the nobility of our just cause shall be recognized in full."

—Julia de Burgos

THE KINGDOM

I, Makandal

I shall be Makandal
a warrior transformed in whatever gender
is necessary
to dethrone this racism
that renders us deeply at fault
at a loss
at such misery
haunting us and humiliating us
I shall dethrone white folk who
paint their faces,
those who still mock
my ethnicity
my race
my color
my big Palesian thick lips

my Mozambican and Julia-de-Burgos skin
my thighs are a Quimbamba
a Tembamdoumbah[1] stroking the machete
to sever blackface in one move

I shall be Makandal
a warrior transformed
carnivalesque
a mosquito swirling over the racist
king, president, or ruler,
a lethal sting
so he won't paint himself no more
so he won't mock no more
so he can understand the pain caused
first, by his chains
then, by laughing fruitlessly at
my destabilizing existence

I shall be Makandal
and my domain shall be this homeland of
discrimination and inequality
which I shall turn anti-racist
abolitionist
because our lives are riding on this,
on me, on my comrades in arms, on
our children and grandchildren to come
to the kingdom of this world

Tembamdoumbah of the Yolanda

Tembamdoumbah commandeers my thick lips
and carves one of the Antilles on my chest
a slave plantation on every nipple
a whiplash in every heartbeat

a slave ship full of dark mothers
drowning each other
to avert boss and master
to avert sodomy
the destruction of wombs
the labor pains of ten-year-olds

a Caribbean caressing my large *bembes*
Tembamdoumbah, seizing my afro
rescues my ass
these killer hips
of booty-swindling dreams
these willful cheeks
allowing me to become
and to be this Tembamdoumbah
who has comforted
my accosted sadness
who has gloated on the cruelty
of our mockers
on the taunting of those

who do not defend
who do not vindicate
who do not support

I punish those of white skin who oppress
and those of dark skin who sweat complicity
those who imitate the speech of a Black woman
unknown to them
an archaic array of sound
the butt of a joke
noises of the tongue that don't represent me
this Tembamdoumbah doesn't want to be
negroide
she doesn't believe in the black evil[2]
of precious songs

I am Black
I am these ordinarily beautiful *bembas*
I am Black
I am this natural bulky afro
I am relaxingly direct, widened, spread around,
a denouncer
I am nappy curls
sparked by braid grooves
entangled to the rhythm of our drums

raveled escape routes
braids of freedom

I am an Afro-Antillean Toum
of frizzles and nappyness
with rumba, macumba, candomblé,
bámbula
among lines of Afro-Boricuas
I am Calabó
a Bambú deity
a jet-stone hand
a swarthy passionate *prieta* claming the Congo
I am Black Tembamdoumbah, my dear Palés
I am frizzy and pure black, my dear Julia
I am Guillén, Carpentier, Caliban,
Makandal
I am from the Blazing Antillean Street

I, Caliban

Stormy Caliban I am
a new creature
Breast and vagina Caliban
a cannibal of our lips
whose mouth I swallow
along this seesaw
I vomit in tears the desire for
emancipation
I prosper in my fight
I fight against Prospero
for the will to be free
to free all my drowned ancestors
salt statues at the bottom of the ocean
jaws of men and women
who opened their mouths wide
to gulp down the entrails of slavers
and you were a master
and now I am your mistress
I dominate the white skin that obsesses you
I subdue your skin with my sex
I am the overseer
I am the whip, concoction, an iron brand on my flesh
and what am I?
I am babalawo

priestess on an island with no shipwrecks
with no castaways
I shall obtain my revenge
upon reaching orgasm
observing my triumph
as I revel in your destruction

prospering amid these winds
swallowing this storm so I can free
my own

I am Caliban
Calibana
Canibalia
Caribbean
your heart lays raw between my fangs
it now descends tender down my throat

Yelidá

that burning in Quisqueyan mouths
is the scattered salt
the raw open wound
and a fleeting tear
against the twist of the spine

another whiplash
and I swear to take my revenge
to become strong
to learn your language
bamboozle you with my voodoo
magic in an Orisha chant
a spell in Ashanti dissonance

that woman-Island
a hoyden devoted to a dark body
defiant
half-cast
mouth of a white woman among black *bembas*
eyelashes dreaming in Togo and Benin
in Sierra Leone, Brazil,
Colombia, Cuba
a biracial poem

a mixed-race verse
a polyethnic Antillean island
you are my Ayti
you are Hispaniola
you are the one who rebels

two mythologies of blood
Damballá
Queddó
Badagris
Legba and Ogun
kiss my delicious voodoo
while among our Caribbean garden
run the puerile Lilliputians
from the snow
the Hyperborean elves from the sleigh
and the reindeer
the Black girl
the blonde hair
the Norwegian beach
One day Afro-Antillean and one day not
white on the others
one before
another before
one after

one parenthesis
another after
an end

a spider soul for the complicit male
Yelidá of the spasm
Yelidá of the way
Yelidá of her womb
slayer of the wind lost between
the teeth
bush and burning
in humid humidity

Creed

I believe in Alejo Carpentier
almighty
creator of the kingdom of this world
of all things visible and invisible
I believe in his cosmos
in this parallel universe
in the reincarnation of karmas,
chakras, and namaste
in his Foucauldian pendulum
and in the wit of the struggle
in protest
in denouncement
in not declining
in the screams that are not extinguished
until justice is found
in the crucifixion of traitors
who steal from the pleb
from the people oppressed by the empire
from the women assassinated by
male chauvinism

I believe in his only Son, Makandal
herbalist redeemer and messiah
hero of magic and voodoo

I believe in the paradise of his *manigua*
in his *palenque*
in his *quilombo*
and from that tangle he shall come
to judge living and dead
enslaved and enslavers
masters and abolitionists
bosses and whiplashers
sodomizers of infants
wet nurses, leaders, and *malinches*
Makandal you are. . . god of light, light
of light, true god of the true god,
engendered and mutilated,
whose are is not
of the same nature as the
Father, for whom all has been created
Makandal you shall be; Makandal I shall be;
he who, for us humans and for our freedom,
descended from heaven
and is sitting to the right of the Father;
and shall return in glory to judge
traitors of the nation and those who refused the machete
and his kingdom shall have no end
I believe in the tempest
in Shakespeare and his children of words
conceived at the warmth of a

rowdy and force-winded Caribbean
cannibal goddess
designer of the screams on my throat
of the abuse of Black bodies
of the mockery by whites who paint their skin
I believe in Prospero, Montaigne, and Ariel
a trinity usurping duchies
sons of kings who make love to Miranda
in the promises to Naples
in the pierced nipples of
homophobes
and the cruel ornament distinguishing the
head of racists
born on the fields of Puerto Rico
landowners and heirs with orange crops
white-haired heads in Castañer
white skin withered before
a plethora of coffee plantations
powerful skins
abusive skins

I believe in witch mother Sycorax,
desiring a son and yearning a father
creator of Heaven and the Earth
who shall crush Trínculo
within my dreams of justice

by the deed and the grace of the holy spirit of
African god Orula

I believe in our holy lady of menses
and her clots
I believe in her pushing of red divinity
that shall drown the oppressors in the
sea of vaginal blood
I believe in a kiss on my glans that is my clitoris
and in that my subjects must caress
my testicular ovaries
so I can silence the mouths of the intolerant

I believe in the contaminated people of Peñuelas
in Tito Kayak[3]
in prisonless political inmates
who go to work every day
for minimum wage
I believe in the students
who suffer under the power
of Pontius Pilate Rosselló
and in the duel for the people of this island
who have been massacred, killed, and
buried according to scripture
who descended into the hell of
an oversight management board[4]

and who on the third day shall resurrect
with their machetes
I shall climb to the heavens
I shall kiss my loves
in polyamory junction
and shall sit with my legs open
with my vagina in the wind
at the right hand of god our father
not-at-all mighty
and shall pour one single baptism
from my hole
over the faces who desire it so
to redeem their sins
and this reign shall also have no end

I believe in Nicolás Guillén, in Llorens Torres,
in Palés Matos, and Corretjer
in the Holy Spirit incarnate in Julia de Burgos
in the holy Church of the four-story country[5]
whose main pillars are Lolita Lebrón
Albizu Campos, Rafael Cancel Miranda,
and Oscar López Rivera

I believe in communion with the saints
in Hostos, Betances, and Rodríguez de Tió
in absolving the sins implied in

giving away our beaches to privatization
to the interests of the wealthy
to banks, hotels, and imperial militia
I believe in the resurrection of the flesh
the conversion of this hallway into the
Republic of Puerto Rico
and the life of the future world
Amen

Goddess Save Thee, Yemoja

Goddess save thee, Yemoja
full of ashe
the iyalawo is with thee
blessed are your daughters who take justice
in their own hands
and blessed is the fruit of your ocean-river
Oshun

Holy Yemoja
mother of goddesses
indulger of every form of love
of all languages and hives of lips
of every female who loves another female

Hail Yemoja Most Pure
sanctified for raising our daughters and sons
and teaching them to return the blow of the
drunk husband
the bully
the abuser
thou are full of bullets
and knives
ready to apply your justice

pray for us orishas, Obatala
Orunmila, mother and father
gods of the holy hermaphroditism
Legba and the transexual angels
now and at the hour
of our freedom
of our civil disobedience
of our devotion to our country
of our Boricua flag
Amen

The Day Fidel Died

The day Fidel died
my country fed on toxic ash
The sea waves in Peñuelas
swayed red and foamy
foreseeing lung cancer
awaiting asphyxiation due to asthma
awaiting the children who shall be born
with leukemia or lupus
all the mothers' wombs
are spontaneously abortive
the entire cropland is contaminated
the entire water streams and springs
laid waste

The day Fidel died
my country was ruled
by a Fiscal Oversight Board
we played at celebrating democratic elections
adrift and without determination
we were still a colony
a shameful crestfallen territory
populated by valiant fighters
who do not fight too much
who pay tribute to the North

to its music, its netflix, its mcdonald's, its Trump,
who praise all things white and blond
who care for blue eyes
who yearn for black Friday and scorn
native tribes

The day Fidel died
Oscar López Rivera was still
shamefully imprisoned
we wrote him songs, poems, stories
we signed release petitions addressed to the Empire
we behave like obedient lambs
nobody orchestrated an escape plan
to blow up his cell
exchanging bullets while fleeing
we sang the hymn of the bowing lamb
we criticized Cuban exiles
we did not relate to their happiness
or their pain
we mocked the celebrations in Havana
and the grieving and their swift mourning

And yet
the day Fidel died
you kissed me
and I promised you hugs in my areolas

you ashed my mouth
an orgasmic wheezing baptized us
ethereal
I drank you
you consumed me
we swore amnesia before months lost
we started anew, from the beginning. . .

#TheDayOscarWasFreed

I live in a barrio
the thugs call *Cacolina*
I listen to screams as if celebrating
among the neighbors
I am decorating the shower
my new shower curtains
the ornaments are white and red
they read: *Love*
I want to surprise my wife
me
a woman married to another
a little prince married to his fox
a display case of monarch butterflies
orange lepidoptera
details of a woman in love

Then my sister Glory calls me
I pause the amazon music channel:
Héctor Lavoe's "Aguanile"
Glory, overcome with tears, tells me
To hear the phrase
"Oscar is free"
from her lips

before anyone else's
has been a gift

I thank life
for giving me so much

Then I call Zu
and we cry

This is what I am doing now
on the day Obama granted freedom
to Boricua Patriot Oscar López Rivera

Guabancex

I'll use the name
I'll use it in your cleavage
I'll name your navel
carbon-colored hips
Guabancex
you, the only *cemí* Taína
included in Fray Ramón Pané's
"Account on the Antiquities of the Indians"
You, Guabancex,
I'll summon you
to taste you
to dilute you
I shall baptize you on the rumor
and my scream of possession
I shall be Inriri Cahuvial
like the myth
like Corretjer
I'll be "fireflies fluttering over a mirror"
I'll be "a gust who is now not just wind"
I'll be "two wings, and with the ones,
and with the beak of the woodpecker"[6]
I shall turn you into a human deity
in wind and water untamable
swirling breeze piercing the hole

in my wooden womb
I have drilled your perforation
I have pricked it like a beaked bird
in your auburn glory to your hands,
Guabancex
glory to your wrath, to your storms in my breasts
praise our homeland-mouth
praise our homeland-tongue
our homeland-kiss
praise
we'll be two women furious mothers
of Juracán
we shall create a child in raw flesh
we shall be the river Corozal,
of the golden legend
we shall make the current drag gold,
we shall make the current drag blood

Calling you Gertrudis

let me call you Gertrudis
for your boldness
your confrontation
your words
your feminism
your valor
are out of this world

let me tell you that you form my constellation
of female warriors
tribal painted huntresses
opposing ablation
opposing prima nocte
opposing alpha males
hymens as trophies
bearing children as a mandate
you are a valkyrie favoring the light of freedom
delivering abortion to those who desire it so

let me call you Avellaneda
for your abolitionism sets the example
it becomes a warm hug
a fierce battle on a cold night
a transmutation of an idealist dream

so I can free myself
so I can infuse courage in others
Black *parejeras*[7] like me
in others who shall become rulers
female presidents of my Island archipelago
who shall be beheaded by the corrupt
I shall paint my face yellow
wage war
cut heads off
eradicate racist languages
I will become La Albizu
of a new era
I shall be La Filiberta
I shall be La Oscar
I will become an herbalist
clitoric babalawo
santera with a harem of men kissers
an orgy of polyamorous women
space of creation
ancestral history
Artivist polygamy
Afrodiasporic mercenary
Dahomey African soldier
Black strategist from Benin
Senegalese sniper
Ghanese amazon

Anaïs Nin
Frida Kahlo
Simone de Beauvoir
Sab
Carlota
Queen Nanny
Juana Agripina
I, Makandal

ancestral Black women
of my mutilated and restituted empire
the freethinking women
of my oppressed and rescued universe
they salute you, Gertrudis Gómez de Avellaneda

Glory

Glory to the Father, Pedro Albizu Campos

Glory to the Son, Commander Filiberto Ojeda Ríos

Glory to the Trinity and Holy Ghostess,
Isabelita Rosado, Rafael Cancel
Miranda, and Lolita Lebrón

As it was in the beginning, now, and
forever, for ever more

Ashe

Litanies

Juana Agripina of Ponce
pray for us women
Black Juana Díaz
pray for us women
Mulata Soledad
pray for us women
Carlota Lucumí of Cuba
pray for us women
Queen Nanny of Jamaica
pray for us women
Luiza Mahin of Brazil
pray for us women
Guerrera Yennega
pray for us women
Taytu Betul of Ethiopia
pray for us women
Nehanda Nyaksikana
pray for us women
Yaa Asantewaa, Ashanti queen
pray for us women
Nzinga Mbande of Angola
pray for us women
Muhumusa of Uganda
pray for us women

Priestess Kaigirwa
pray for us women
Tarenorerer, Black woman of Australia
pray for us women
servicewomen of Dahomey
pray for us women
amazons from the kingdom of Benin
pray for us women
Borinken[8] Maroons
pray for us women
Antillean sucklers
pray for us women
wet nurses and nannies
pray for us women
Black child bearers
pray for us women
Black women avengers
pray for us women
Sojourner Truth
pray for us women
Harriet Tubman
pray for us women
Rosa Parks
pray for us women
Assata Shakur
pray for us women

Angela Davis
pray for us women
Toussaint Louverture
pray for us women
Saint Domingue
pray for us women
Ayiti
pray for us women
Puerto Rico
land of Borinken[8], where I was born
pray for us women

Thunderlips

And thus I rebuke the villain:
yo sería borincana
aunque naciera en la luna[9]
I also yell that I grew up
that I am over it, that I became strong
that him bullying me by calling my hair *pelo malo*
no longer burdens me, no longer hurts me,
no longer pierces
that his offenses and grievances
wire hair, rudderfish mouth
you black thing, stinky *prieta*
big lips, the color of shit
no longer touch me;
for I am like the moon; I am the sea, and I am
from the mountain; I am a chimera in song
a crystal of tears, Puerto Rican with nothin'
but with no affliction
I am Thunderlips, more than a girl's
nickname, more than a suffered insult
a superheroine, a fighter for
identity and justice
I would be a proud Black Borincana
even if I were born on the moon

The Sign of the Cross

In the name of the nationalist
Black flag, our Mother

and of the Daughter, the white cross in the middle

and in the rebellious Spirit of the Ponce
Masacre, Aurora Domingo de Ramos Street

where hundreds of black flags
with white crosses were tainted red

fell on the ground, and impunity
reigned

Amen

Haitian Creole

Bonjou Atemis, Bondye fanm, Yemaya
Konplè nan Ashe
babalawo la rete nan mitan nou
beni pitit fi nou yo ki pran jistis nan men pwòp yo
ak Benediksyon pou fwi a nan oseyan Ochun ou

santa Yemaya
manman deyès
consentidora nan tout lanmou
nan tout lang ak nich nan bouch
chak fi ki renmen yon lòt fanm

Purisima Ave Yemayá
mete apa yo si nou ogmante pitit fi nou ak pitit gason
epi anseye yo fè grèv tounen bwè mari
maltratador
abizè
plen nan bal
ak lam
prete pou ekzekisyon

lapriyè pou mwen tou orishas
Obatala
Orula manman ak papa

bondye moun peyi ki apa pou èrmafrodit ak transganr
 zanj Bondye yo Eleguá
kounye a ak nan lè a
pou libète
dezobeyisans sivil
Defansè
livrezon nan peyi nou an
ak Borincana drapo nou an
Amèn

Yoruba

Kabiyesi Goddess, Yemaya
Full ti Ashe
awọn babalawo wà pẹlu nyin
sure fun awọn ọmọbinrin nyin ti o ya idajọ sinu ara
wọn ọwọ
ati ibukun ni awọn eso ti rẹ Oshun òkun

Santa Yemaya
iya oriṣa
consentidora ti gbogbo fẹ
ti gbogbo awọn ede ati swarms ti ète
gbogbo obinrin ti o fẹràn miran obinrin

Purisima Ave Yemayá
mimọ nipa igbega awọn ọmọbinrin wa ati awọn ọmọ
ki o si kọ wọn lati lu pada mu yó ọkọ
maltratador
abuser
ti o kún fun awako
ati abe
yawo fun ipaniyan

gbadura fun wa orishas
Obatala

Orula iya ati baba
awọn orịṣa awọn mimọ hermaphrodite ati transgender
angẹli Eleguá
bayi ati ni wakati
ti ominira
abele aigboran
defenders
oba ti wa Ile-Ile
ati ki o wa flag Borincana
Amin

Of This World

Our Father

Our Father

who were in the Orlando massacre
and did nothing

Hallowed by remaining silent and
unmovable for reasons all
your followers know,
but the rest of us
don't . . .

Our Father, whom we suppose
comforts on this day the fathers
and mothers of those who lost their lives
that night. . .

Our Father who hides in
heaven, and there remains, and who
from there has us believe that you send
for people of the Earth

You say you miss them, and they were slaughtered . . .
on your behalf

Our Father who from His kingdom
enchants so many, making them believe
that everything is your will, that everything is your
purpose, that nothing goes unnoticed
before you, and that we are your imperfect,
barely rational creation according to your
design . . .

Our Father who has seen me tongue kiss
another woman like me,
who knows my beginning and my end,
my origin and my omega, my alpha and
my orgasms, my lesbian sexual urgency

and that of my homosexual, bisexual, transexual,
intersexual, and pansexual
siblings. . .

Hallowed be my patience, tolerance, and
acceptance of you, Father.

In the name of the 49 dead at the
Pulse massacre, in Orlando, I hope
they can forgive you, Amen

I Did Not Come to Pick Up My Son

I did not come to pick up my son
like in kindergarden
after preparing his lunchbox
or waiting in the lunchroom
making sure no one bothered him
like a privilege of an anxious father
needing to be in front of the fence
to see him come out safe
to be there in case a giant attacked him
making him cry
mocking his weak muscles
or his girly voice

I did not come to call for my child
as when I visited him at the dressing room
for his first play
or at his premiere with the dance team
knowing that he was suffering
seemingly searching inside the fruit basket
for some rose hidden by his mother
the ones only he enjoyed
in secret
to avoid harassment
frustration

funny looks, and crude humiliation
of so many ignorant onlookers

I did not come to identify my son
as when he marched in his first
communion
disguising his friendship with some
altar boy
concealing his colorful clothes
the suitcase with flamboyant makeup
wigs, hats, and stoles,
glitter, and leather high heels

I did not carry my dead son
as in the Vatican's *Pietà*
I did not have the courage
I did not go to his body
I did not come to his face
nor his tearful lashes facing the pain
of bullets
I did not come to his trembling arms
lacking my blessing
nor to the hole in his dying neck
missing a crown of flowers
I did not see his lips uttering
lament

I did not recite in his ear the prayer
of the guardian angel
I did not say amen with him
I did not twist and turn upon his lack of pulse
upon his dying blinking eyes
facing his last breath
I did not want to be there
I did not look for him at the morgue
I did not get him out of that purple freezer
I did not pick him up to kiss his forehead
I did not burry him
shame is to blame
that discotheque is to blame
the murderer is to blame
I am to blame
and in the end
I did not go because I want to still think of him
as being alive . . .

Act 54[10]

we shall not cry victory
nor recognize your violence
and my victimization
it is not prodigal

knowing now that
the arrival of the police is legit
to help me
to imprison you
turning me into an official victim
a legal martyr

testifying before puppets
in a system of coxcombs
an island parody
who arms in arms intones that
I'd be Borincano even if I were born on the
moon
while patiently waiting
for washington
and its egalitarian handouts
is not at all glorious. . .
we shall not cry victory

Seismologic Scale

my diverse hand
my diverse fist
my diverse arm
variation of colors
and of one flag

I confess I love a woman
her round plump breasts
fallen with the nobility of the years
I confess her nipples craze me

before all of this
the vigor of my crimes
against any christ
is less than 3.2

I confess to have incited
achieving a fierce fellatio
while I practice the immorality of
cunnilingus
within a mixture of loving aromas
an atypical triangle
whose dimension rises to a moderate
5.6

if I reveal that I fantasize
with the sexy intellectual Lizza Fernanda
her carnal shapes
her verbal axioms
her elocution
the quake elevates its waves: 7.3

if on the contrary
I groan
rant
claim
rumble
roil
unleash
and scream to the memory of Jorge Steven
the devastation would cause great damage
my condemnation
becomes an event
never before recorded
my wrath destroys the intolerant
bible-thumping haters
Cain-impersonating assassins
and human history
has never registered
indignation
of such magnitude

wrath is as intense as this
yet love is otherwise

you and I have long since
overcome this scale

Map to the Clitoris

the first thing you need is this:
innocent hands
washed in the blood of the lamb
and the little animal is around the groin
or soaked in the sap
of a menstruating sheep

the second thing
you need is to be catholic
apostolic or roman
marian
charismatic or adventist
mormon
evangelical or pentecostal
a follower of kardec
orisha
wicca
babalwo or pagan

to be one of these
and also shy
or alluring
feminine or rough
it doesn't matter, it's all the same

I promise to bring you out of the closet
before grandparents
brothers, sisters,
aunts-in-law,
gossiping neighbors,
and cousins that cuddle

I'll be your first
your conqueror
the untamable one
and I'll provide you with the precise cartography
so you may follow
a map to a well-licked clit
sucked with gusto

you'll never be lost
in these avenues
I promise!
and then you may give
the right directions
to all that may be relished
to the next woman

A Poem for Wanda

have you ever felt, wanda,
the tremor of a mouth
posing at the top
of a female glans?

we also have
this promontory

this cloud of flesh
center of palpitations
of kleitós, klitos, cleitós
a Greek word, wanda,
become enlightened

licking an inferior labium, wanda,
and thinking about it in phoenician
thinking about it in latin or arameic
thinking about it from etymology
recreated to communicate things
to come closer via this interaction
and tremble one another
shake you
suck on the small mound
and recall

the academy of language of any country
rise to lick the tongue of any woman
or better yet
the taste buds of the beloved women
follow to the letter
the words in a dictionary
a truly venerable book

royal
academy
royal academy
word
word becoming flesh
and living among us
sanctified words
more sacred that that other book
you misrepresent

can you find the button
that makes us burst, Wanda,
has someone
has some time activated yours before?

some man
some woman

some man looking like a woman
some woman looking like a man
or some intersexual sibling
with vagina and penis?

has anyone taught you how to milk
the plummy breasts
of an excited woman, Wanda?
did you father explain
what masturbating is?
or did you mother tell you
about the virtues of remaining a virgin
on the front end
while surrendering your oiled booty?

have you been told about the delight
of not having to tell
between anus and vulva
do you know how to aromatize
a menstruating vagina?

anti-christ wanda
pathetic apostle
of the new inquisition
eat your heart out!

Pink Oubao Moin

Celebrate a multicolor legend
Celebrate a current and a rainbow
Celebrate and then another hate crime
Praise!

We awake in agony with another
Jorge Steven
We awake in tears and expectation
We wake up with branches spouting
blood
Praise!

The Black man, the Native woman, the *jabao*,[11]
the white woman, the mixed-race man, the dark-skin
  man,
they break their backs
Their branded bodies show a pink triangle scar
And the horror and the abuse persist
Praise!

Glory to those lesbian hands for they work.
Glory to those bisexual hands for they work.
Praise!

Glory to those transexual hands for they work.
Glory to those transgender hands.
Glory to those diverse hands.
For they knead the homeland.
Praise!

The homeland of all hands!
For them and for their homeland, praise!
Praise!
Pink hands that build and
from them a new free homeland shall emerge

Public Places

"Your silence will not protect you."
—Audre Lorde

I am a respectful dike
any displays of affection
I keep them only for the decorum
of the couch

so dictates our creed that we must be strict
do not make out with another woman in public
none of that piercing her lips with your tongue
as if anchoring a longboat
over the sea at Caracoles Cay
nor massaging her gums with the tip of your tongue
crystal-clear water at Caja de Muertos
not to mention closing your eyes
embracing her waist
let me tighten in her stead
the rudders or helms at El Alambique
at La Parguera or El Faro
do not slide your hands below her back
nor stick your fingers inside her fleshy
piggy bank

as if we were slow dancing at a *marquesina*[12]
or at a Dorado or Isla Verde public beach
or a *bachata* under the cloudless sun
as couples or adulterers,
they who love each other

I am a respectful Black woman
may the desire to write
about truth and oppression
never lead me to me point at the white man
or his grandparents
those who surely enslaved mine
none of that desire to improve my race
or hinder its advance
or write poems about equality
or lines about prejudice
one should not upset grandchildren
who inherited the status quo
with deceitful memories

all hair shall be straightened
none of those nappy afro
I shall uncolor my skin
avoid suntan lotion at Piñones
at any cost

the unoppressed must be respected
those who have never experience
please be a respectable Black woman
a worthy and moral dyke

excuse me
are you offended by the scaffold,
the pillory, the whiplashes,
a white penis introduced
in all black vaginas?
excuse me for reminding you,
you, who have worked so hard
to forget.

are you offended by our kiss
while you hide your homophobia
after watching lesbian porn?
how insensitive of me!

excuse me
I forget that for you to be at ease
you believe that we don't get it on

I repeat my creed
we must be strict
don't forget to be white

as white as possible
don't forget to behave as a hetero
as straight as possible
you are expected to be in your best
behavior
in public places
do not renege on this
don't instruct others who do not
question
those who don't read
those who don't know their history and don't
want to know it
those who remain unwise or
ignorant
those who defend refusing to fight to seem
or resemble being white
or heterosexual
which is the same thing in the end

I Confess

marriage proposal for Zulma

I confess that I write poems on
the blank pages of fiction books
and later rip them out
I confess that I paint all
my toenails and that I like
to walk in flipflops
I confess that I have 148 versions of
The Little Prince
one in Arabic I don't understand
another one in Hungarian
German, Italian, Portuguese, French, and
several bootleg editions
I confess that I have a Little Prince
tattooed on the nipple of my dark right breast
I confess that this is a lie;
the tattoo rests on my left shoulder
I confess that I swore never to marry again
and now that equality may be celebrated soon
I will tie the knot with a woman whom I've never
asked to marry me
I confess that I like your mouth
the smell of your neck and the match

our engagement rings make
she and I are a blank book
we shall write together
tales and poems of high erotic content
I confess that I've never bowed down to no one
and that this is the first time. . .
So, Zulma
My darling
You, the Fox to my Little Prince,
will you marry me?

Perigee

Kiss my perigee
the bellybutton of overgrown waves
blessing your face
Take me at an angle closest
to your mouth
and grab this throat with you hand closed
with your bite of lunar lips
Tie the ropes
Move me around this garden of pheromones
dripping
like roses transformed into oceans
flooding your gasping skin
Make me your supermoon
Turn me into your orbit and dry the tide in these eyes
that have cried so much for you
Undress this crater
and land on the deep folds of my moon
the ones that pump blood
beating storms before upon your return

Two Equals

a poem invitation for the 2015 collective wedding

Loving between two equals
in the passionate uproar between woman and woman
between man and man
Hugging as you wait for the right moment
Roaring in every direction that it's time
this is our moment. . .

we are conjured by being one single flesh
we want to promise each other tickles,
breakfast, vacations
we desire to swear each other gentleness,
tears of joy, tenderness. . .

I am the first grape of the vine
You are the agave harvest
Together we are a sunset before
the sea at El Morro
We both are a hug with the essence of
coffee and *tembleque*,
two corners of the lips, two bouquets of eyelashes
the passionate desire for uttering
in our Island of Enchantment

"I love you; I take you as my husband"
"I adore you; I take you as my wife"

Relatives, friends, and acquaintances in Puerto Rico
we invite you to join us in this legal union
our liberation, our equality, and our justice
on Sunday, July 19, 2015, at 1:00 pm
in Old San Juan

Where Are the Pillows?

alea iacta est

What do you need to be happy?, you ask,
I eagerly answer:
a lover that gives me pillows

a soft, firm pillow
with memory foam or latex
for remembering strictly what is necessary
and forgetting that I have no ring

a feather pillow
anti-allergenic, without asthma
for sleeping on one side
flying face up
entwine my skin with another
certain that someone will understand me
without psychoanalysis

a pillow that doesn't take me to extremes
nor tries to diagnose me
that understands Einstein's equation
Hawking's radiation
the eleven dimensions

a house built by Kepler
the vice of a keyboard

a pillow so that my neck
remains beautifully horizontal
aligned with the rest of my untrusting spine
vertebral posture injured
by halfway promises
or open pain
so dreadfully open
without hope for redemption

Those who sleep on their side
often require dreams and French kisses
on frank mouths
a sexy whistle of the tongue
tears and snot that don't choke you
when summoned;
thicker pillows are preferred
with the proper timely apology
that doesn't throw past mistakes in your face
nor remind the day and time when you were a victim
and not the aggressor

A soft, fine pillow
that makes you sleep face down

may avoid what cold therapy commands
the ones that hospitalize grievances
against pampering
the consequences of an inadequate posture
will bring lack of rest and forgetfulness
a stiff neck
morning contractures
or even eventful endings;
if you move too much and change posture
a pillow of medium firmness
would be ungrateful
it will not value your efforts
will make you cry during traffic jams
while you brush your teeth facing the mirror
and in lady's room at the office
you will lose your head little by little
and will snore bombastically crazy

I Became a Mother

celebrating Mother's Day 2015

I became a mother on the day I pushed your
swarms of quilty arms
weighing seven point six in October. I became
a mother with your extension
emerging from me, long and
merciful, on the rocking chair of your
twenty-one inches; hand grabbing
my thumbs; legs kicking like
a tambour on my bellybutton, ruckus of
stretch marks drawn over my torso as if
you were a female homo erectus threading
images inside an occipital
cave; my Edenic and prehistoric
uterus now baptized in the
blessing of your transit. I became
a mother at the throat, upon beholding you as
you beheld me, when those asteroid eyes like
the little prince set over mine, and I
choked on the intensity of
your mastery, of your dexterity, of the conquest
you already achieved over me, in
those bare first twenty-one

seconds of life. You pulsed and declared
me Whole. I became an
Orionid fireball. You ripped my cubital
line with fierce ability so that
from that moment I would
defend you Unique, Potent, Fierce. That
you are—a fierce daughter has
made me the mother most full of
grace in the galaxy. I am yours, aurora
borealis, ever since that day and
forever.

To my daughter Aurora

Constance Like This

Constance like this
on the mirror's truth
knowing myself bound to your name
knowing you are not alone
and I am more amicable
at this short age staring at you
who already knows your drunken folly
your sad falls
happy stumbles
the blow
a corner crash with reality
because you miss a man
as I will miss a woman
when I grow up
not now;
not under this clouded sky
about to snow
where both of us are strangers
and have found each other
a foul alley
I am Constancia
a girl who perseveres
and this persistence of yours to smile at me
in a barrio that is not yours

neither yours nor mine
that does not talk like you
nor me

resolute,
we agreed to play
or I agreed
because you were quite dizzy
a debutant on the ground
some rough vomiting
the violence of a chewed gullet
dumpster of redcurrants
insolence on the sidewalk
walls aged by fear

I also hide around
fleeing my stepfather
to feel pain here
in this protective alley
of slave eyes picking cotton
where does it hurt, miss, where does it sting,
right in the middle of my dormant people
we played little girl, little girl
where have you been?
gathering flowers to give to the queen
little girl, little girl what she gave she you?

she gave me a verse
as big as my shoe

and you said you were a poet
I gave you my name:
write a poem, miss
with the word Constancia
that's also my name
that's also your name
my second name, you said
for the first one is Julia

and you tried to rise
removing cigarette butts
from your hair
you tried to bend a knee
find support
balance the flask
bottle of magnificent glass
anesthetic for heartaches
katzenjammers
woe, woe, woe —you said— you are nappy
and pure Black
you pointed at my hair
naps in my hair
you caressed my mouth

kinkiness in my mouth
your flat nose is ours

where does it hurt, miss, where does it sting
in the man, pretty Black girl—you whispered
man hurts me
to feel pain here
right in the middle of your slave grandpa
right in the middle of oppressors
shame if he'd been the master
woe, woe, woe

Rebel Julia

Warrior, say the waves
from the sea that bathes you. . .

you were Jane Doe
for a short while
you are and always will be eternity
insurging great surge of Loíza
an untamable troublemaker
woman of values
whom I want to repeat
in my daughters
in the daughters of my daughters

a merger of revolutions you are
a bunch of word arrows you are
a confabulator
with Albizu
Corretjer
Martí
Juan Bosch
a name appearing in FBI files
letters delivering our conscience you are
a fireball of wit

letters sparking fury
that humiliates the lukewarm

And you have the gallant nobility of
sister Spain
And the fierce song of the brave Taíno
you also have

"Blessed be the say in which a woman
be the one to fall defending the freedom
of her homeland
On that day there will be a revolution
in every Puerto Rican home,
and we shall fully recognize
the greatness of our just cause"

Words of an illustrious Julia in 1936
unerasable scars of reckless mark
Julia the rebel
Julia the stoic
Julia the one who I love to pay homage
indomitable woman
disobedient
woman who burns the yearning
to be a feisty bold captain

woman who would be a worker
cutting cane, sweating the workday

people already mutter
that you are a complete Homeland
uprisen in verse
not in your voice: but in mine

Warrior say the bards who
verse your story
No matter if the tyrant treats you with white evil
Poet you shall be with a flag, awards, and glory
Rebel, Great Julia, say the daughters
of freedom

I am Julia and I have returned

I am Julia and I have returned to be born
on February 17
I have returned at Sunrise
to cradle myself to a Song of Simple Truth
I have come at Almost Dawn to love you,
Juan Isidro
but will not follow you to Havana
nor give you my hands and nails
stuck on your back
I shall not shower your neck with kisses
or passion
I will not allow you to give me only
a one-way ticket
to send me to New York with no
ultimatum
fearing that your mother of father
don't want you with me

I am Julia, Black Julia
I am nappy and purely Black
and I have returned to tell you, Juan Isidro
that it is not worth to get drunk
because of you

or because your wife left you
or because you stay with her
or because you lost your entire inheritance

I am Julia, Juan Isidro,
and my Great Loíza River this time
will not be dedicated to your silhouette
I shall be the Julia who wants to be a man
who wants to be the ship's captain
Pentachromy
I shall be the Julia who will know Sor Juana and
Sor Filotea
the one who wants to date all the
men I so desire
while I battle with valiant Boricuas
who care for her Island
who fight for its autonomy, for its
sovereignty, and for the choice of being
I am Julia
the one who founded the army of
the Daughters of Freedom
the one who created poems
and wrote books flirting with Corretjer
I am the Julia de Burgos who is
grateful of teachers

for teaching with gender perspective
even though there are no circular letters
or hollow regulations
I am the Julia who does not want girls
to feel less than a boy
the one who wants all young women to aspire
to be all they yearn for
I am the Julia who wished the best for the homeland
the Julia from the Poem With the Last Tune
Poem of the Eternal Encounter
Poem of Intimate Agony
Poem of My Sleeping Sorrow
Poem to My Unborn Son
Poem For Tears
Poem of My Sail of Anxiety
Poem for My Death

I am Julia de Burgos
And on this return, I know you, Yolanda of mine
you are a verse in my lips, rowdy
Black woman
you are The Winged Flight
the Sails of a Memory
with me, you have been I Was My Own Route
with me, you are the quietest one

I am Julia Constancia
and on this return, I did not die on the street
of no anglosaxon neighborhood
nor suffered pneumonia
cold does not permeate to my bones
because I was laid down on a sidewalk
there is no snow
there is no ice

I am Julia de Burgos of Arroyo Pizarro
of Oliveras Vega and of Cruz Bernal
I am the one who demands: Give Me My Number
Now

Black Flesh

smelling black flesh black blood / biting
blackness / pinching black cheeks /
fondling your black ass / remembering
my blackened mother / obfuscated /
tarnished by perky coal / humming
black lullabies from my black coco grandfather
black *tembleque* / rough *majarete*
hunt the cunt hunt the cunt vegigante eat the cunt
blackest *marrayo* in a scratched mouth /
big thick lips to bite you in piñones /
sleepwalking eyelashes from fucking
you in cataño / isla de cabras beach
punta salinas beach / perla beach /
mouth mumble beach / dark shackle
earring / brown mixed creole nose /
I blacken your crack of wheat-colored
lollypop / blacken my churlish purple
tongue / caress my purple gums
with blackish sugar / trou-kuh-tah
trou-kuh-tah / your black onion / trou-kuh-tah
trou-kuh-tah /your black dick black /
so fine is your sweetest
underground deep / the Cepedas and Ayalas
in every spasm / pamper me

with the free plena / with the free bomba /
with the coconut candy / sweet black thing / a
blue pussy / darkest / all yours /
your black girl / so fine she is /
pizarro I am

Bravado

Italy, 2016

Your mouth
an orchestra directing inconsistency
and learning new ways
of stripping away sanity
if one imagines
the musical fire of its onslaught
or the shivering sounds
where all my madness come from

From that profound kiss
wrapped in the lunar honey
of your face
I see you return. . .
planting the flag
marking your territory among blue roses
tightening your fangs on my neck
an offering

Your mouth
a reef battered by molotov
cocktails
if the demanding sound of your arrival

roars over the tones of the piano
howls on the chords of the cello
moos while burying rhythms of the
chiaroscuro

Meanwhile, the crescendo of your conquest
lands on my moon
like a Roman emperor
like Alexander the Great
la mia ragazza, la mia donna, dolce fidanzata
your bass and contralto lips
offer the exquisite Bravado
the posture
the silhouette
the sovereignty of a jawbone
your army's arrogant tour
before my skin's mapamundi

And you thunder
you yell
like a primitive creature
rubbing its head against my brain
biting the language of
the Hominidae;
both of us shaken
submerged in this ectasis
of a wet dawn

#OccupyMe

I am Octoberian, Octobrerin,
Octobrian, Octoberist. I write
only on the 29th. I menstruate
riding on asteroid b612, bound
to collide with the planet. I agonize
tired of injustice, of exclusion,
fed up with differences—all of them
made up. This is why I write. I whisper
the word *desosirium*[13] on the mouth of the
Little Prince. A whispered denounce, a
quantic ancestral design in which all
parallels, black holes, and supernovas
give me the full and perfect right
of kissing men and women in the mouth,
to bear creatures with a vulva from my
vulva, and hum the songs of Calle 13.

I am a woman who occupies, a Black
woman who occupies, a bisexual who
occupies. I am the denouncer,
the interventor who swaps, who transgresses,
who turns things upside down. Dark skin,
witching eyes, and beguiling lashes. A Puerto Rican
with 29 birthmarks around her body,
a fortune teller's map on every palm of each hand

and not much air in her lungs, reduced by
asthma. I am the opposite sex of the
opposite sex, touched by her own reflection.
I have been born on a new moon by
my only daughter with an austral name.

This is why I write.

Notes

1 (T.N.) Alliteration of "Tembandumba," taken from the female character Tembamdumba de la Quimbamba, a young Afro-Puerto Rican woman from the poem "*Majestad Negra*" (black majesty) by Luis Palés Matos. The poetic voice in the poem admires the young woman's body as she walks down the street, highlighting phenotypical features supposedly ascribed to Black women. *Bembe* is a Puerto Rican variant of *bembo*: a mouth with thick lips, particularly from a person of African descent (*Tesoro Lexicográfico de Puerto Rico: https://tesoro.pr/lema/bembe*).

2 (T.N.): Allusion to Rafael Hernández's renowned song "Preciosa" (precious one) ©1937. The poetic voice questions the use of "negra maldad" ("black evil") as pejorative and racist. The lyrics say: *No importa el tirano te trate con negra maldad.* (literally): "Despite the tyrant treating you with black evil." The song is considered by many as Puerto Rico's second national anthem. Rafael Hernández was well-known an Afro-Puerto Rican songwriter in the Hispanic world.

3 (T.N.): Puerto Rican political activist famous for climbing into tall structures and planting a Puerto Rican flag at the top.

4 (T.N.): Fiscal Oversight and Management Board. Political entity created by Act of Congress on 2016 (PROMESA Act), for the purpose of restructuring Puerto Rico's public debt. The board has power over the Government and Legislature of Puerto Rico regarding financial organizations and institutions. Every budget and financial decision must have the approval of this FOMB.

5 Allusion to *El país de lo cuatro pisos* (the four-story country), an essay by José Luis González published in 1980 (Ediciones Huracán). The author proposes Puerto Rico as a four-story building, each floor represents a stage in our cultural history.

6 Verses from "Inriri Chauvial" ("woodpecker" in the Taíno language), written by Juan Antonio Corretjer.

7 (T.N.): Puerto Rican slang for a haughty, snobby, pedantic, cocky, arrogant, sumptuous person. https://tesoro.pr/lema/parejero-ra

8 (T.N.): Indigenous name given to Puerto Rico by the Taínos.

9 "I shall be Borincana, even if I were born on the moon" is an allusion to "Un Boricua en la luna," a famous poem by Juan Antonio Corretjer.

10 Act No. 54 of August 15, 1989, as amended; "Domestic Abuse Prevention and Intervention Act," enacted by the Commonwealth of Puerto Rico's Government.

11 Word used in the Hispanic Caribbean to denote a light-skinned Afrodescendant.

12 (T.M.): A *marquesina* is car park or terrace typical of Puerto Rican houses, commonly used to shelter the family vehicle. It is a structure adjoined to the house, usually gated, and leading to the rear yard in the back. In the 1980s and 1990s, it was common to host birthday celebrations and high-school dance parties in empty *marquesinas*.

13 (T.N.): *Desosirio* is portmanteau whereby Yolanda Arroyo Pizarro blends the words *desolación* (desolation) and *delirio* (delirium). The word has been previously translated by David Caleb Acevedo as *desosirium* in his rendering of Arroyo Pizarro's *Caparazones* (*Caparaces*). I prefer to use his rendering here.

YOLANDA ARROYO PIZARRO is a Puerto Rican writer. She has published several books that denounce and set forth passionate approaches, fostering a debate on Afro-identity and sexual diversity. She directs the Department of Afro-Puerto Rican Studies, a performance project in Creative Writing hosted by the Casa Museo Ashford, in San Juan. Yolanda also founded the Black Ancestral Women Lectureship in response to the call issued by UNESCO to celebrate the International Decade for People of African Descent. Arroyo Pizarro was invited by the United Nations Remembering Slavery program to address the intersection of women, slavery, and creativity in 2015. Her collection of short stories *las Negras*, winner of the Puerto Rico PEN Club National Award in Short-Story Fiction (2013) explores the limited historical paths of female characters who defy the hierarchies of power. *Caparazones*, *Lesbofilias*, and *Violeta* are some of the novels where she explores transgression from an openly visible lesbianism. Arroyo Pizarro also won the National Short-Story Prize awarded by the Institute of Puerto Rican Culture (in 2012 and 2015), and the Institute of Puerto Rican Literature National Prize in 2008. Her work has been translated into German, French, Italian, English, Portuguese, and Hungarian.

ALEJANDRO ÁLVAREZ NIEVES Writer, translator, and professor. He is the author of the poetry anthologies *El proceso traductor* (AC, 2012) and *Quiebre de armas* (Trabalis, 2018), in addition to the short story collection *Galería de comandos* (Alayubia, 2019). He was the general programmer of San Juan's Festival de la Palabra until 2018. Prof. Álvarez Nieves has translated for several literary magazines, such as *World Poetry* and *Poetry Review,* as well as international publishers, such as Temas de Hoy. His Spanish translation of *Wild Beauty, Belleza Salvaje,* by Ntozake Shange (Atria, 2017), earned him the International Latino Book Award in 2018, in the Spanish translation category. Alejandro Álvarez Nieves is an assistant professor in the Graduate Program in Translation at the University of Puerto Rico, Río Piedras Campus.

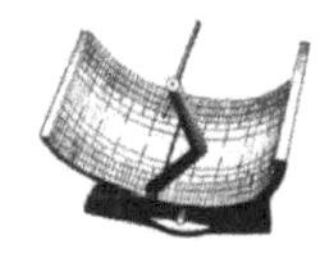

(l)as Negras

SUNDIAL HOUSE

(l)as Negras

Yolanda Arroyo Pizarro

SUNDIAL HOUSE NEW YORK • PHILADELPHIA

Primera edición en español: 2016

La diagramación y el diseño de la portada estuvieron a cargo de Lisa Hamm.
La imagen de la portada es obra de Scherezade García: "Stories of Wonder," de la serie *Early Encounters* (2019). Acrílico, pigmentos, carboncillo y aerosol sobre lienzo (72" x 48"). Colección privada.
Fotografía de William Vázquez.
Correctora de pruebas: Lizdanelly López Chiclana.

ISBN: 979-8-9879264-2-0

Contenido

El Reino

De este mundo

Escribir *las Negras*

YOLANDA ARROYO PIZARRO

LOS ESCLAVOS eran muy felices. Eran personas muy felices siendo esclavos.

Esas fueron las primeras oraciones que aprendí en tercer grado, expresadas por nuestra maestra de Historia y Estudios Sociales, Sor Rosario. Al parecer la monja necesitaba a toda costa que nos aprendiéramos aquel lavado de cerebro porque nos lo hizo recitar de memoria, al menos a mí y a Juan Carlos, el otro niño negro de mi salón. Fuimos el ejemplo, seleccionados para que los demás niños de Cataño, más aclarados, más blancuzcos, más claritos, menos negros que nosotros, entendieran que el mito de las tres razas en Puerto Rico no era tan mito, que era real y que junto al endiosamiento de saberse uno blanco español (según la monja), y junto a la altivez de reconocerse uno como trigueño taíno de pelo lacio (según la monja), había que sentir igual o más orgullo—nunca superioridad—por ser descendiente de esclavo negro africano con pelo malo (según la monja).

Pero yo era *hija* de mi abuela Petronila, un ser como pocos, quien había parido a una nieta subversiva, llevándole la contraria a la biología, a la madre naturaleza y a deidades de todo tipo. Aquella crianza abuela-nieta había desembocado en la creación de un ser que refutaría todo lo que se le parara de frente hasta satisfacer las más polémicas curiosidades. "*Eres un espíritu de contradicción*", vociferaba abuela Petronila molesta mientras me corría entre gallinas y gallos por el patio de la casa en barrio Amelia. Casi siempre presumía de mí, pero de vez en cuando se exasperaba porque a veces su propia obra se le iba en contra. "*Nunca te quedas callada, eres contestona. Tienes la boca llena de malacrianzas. Ese será tu infortunio*", recitaba furibunda a su Ópera Prima.

Abuela Toní—diminutivo de Petronila Cartagena Mitchen, nacida el 5 de diciembre de 1912—articulaba toda posible comunicación del modo más inteligente y brillante, nunca antes atestiguado por mí. En idioma español de enciclopedia Cumbre y su inglés conversacional de octavo grado, sabía inculcar y convencer, con lo cual fue suficiente para convertirla en secretaria de la Puerto Rican Cement hasta la aparición del consorte más galante de la comarca, mi abuelo Saturnino Pizarro Costoso.

Con aquella articulación tan frondosa e hipnotizante defendería posturas, calmaría altercados, rebatiría opiniones sobre el pasado y el futuro del archipiélago, amonestaría al resto de matriarcas de la calle Herminio Díaz Navarro y organizaría contubernios vecinales para sobrevivir los huracanes, tan pronto el mar del malecón se salía de la bahía. Ella comparaba al huracán Hugo y al huracán David con el huracán San Ciriaco de 1899, cuyos detalles conocía a la perfección gracias a los cuentos de la *ancestra* Georgina, su madre y bisabuela mía.

Inventé la palabra *Ancestra* una noche mientras escribía relatos en trance. Era 1998 y me encontraba embarazada de mi hija Aurora, unigénita. Escribía para recordar a abuela Petronila, para rescatarla, para traerla de vuelta del Alzheimer que la estaba secuestrando. Inventé *Ancestra* para hablar de mis abuelas, bisabuelas y tatarabuelas. Ya tenía experiencia con palabras inventadas, pues Petronila, abuela materna, ya decía *desosirio*. Miguelina, mi abuela paterna, hablaba además de español e inglés, un poco de alemán y ello la obligaba a "criollizar" algunas expresiones; es decir, inventar la manera de hacernos entender. Las abuelas madamas del vecindario, emigradas de las islitas, me hablaban en francés, creole y swahili. Por tanto, siempre vi natural la mezcla de tiempos verbales, la conjugación de lo inconjugable y hacer parir neologismos.

Por eso cuando me senté a las tres de la madrugada aquella vez, a escribir el primer párrafo de *las Negras* en 2003, supe que quería resaltar el femenino de la negritud. Supe que deseaba que el título de mi libro empezara con la minúscula del artículo y le siguiera la mayúscula del sustantivo.

Quise que la adjetivación de aquel sustantivo, o la sustantivación de aquel adjetivo, fuera protagonista. Fuera *prietagonista*. Por eso en 2003, ante el dolor del fallecimiento de mi abuelamadre, solo me restó entrar en trance . . . escribir las historias que Petronila me había contado, escuchar el dictado de las mujeres de mi casta en la voz de la memoria de mami Toní.

Tengo en la memoria el recuerdo de mi abuela haciéndome estas historias de sus propias abuelas. Las Negras que llegaron en barco, las Negras que labraron la tierra, las Negras que fueron comadronas, las Negras que pavimentaron los caminos, que fueron castigadas, amonestadas, que se vengaron, que envenenaron captores. Abuela me hacía dictados cuando estaba viva, en presencia, en carne y hueso, y luego de fallecida también me hizo dictados en mis sueños, en mis recuerdos, en mis alucinaciones, porque yo alucinaba de tanto llorarla, y de tanto necesitarla, y de tanto extrañarla.

Por eso aquel día de 1978 cuando la monja enseñó la foto del risueño indio taíno y el gallardo conquistador español junto al encadenado y "feliz" africano que llevábamos semanas "aprendiendo" como parte de la historia de nuestra Isla, yo convoqué a mi "espíritu de contradicciones" y altanera articulé a lo Petronila: "*nadie encadenado puede ser feliz*". Acto seguido, el salón estalló en risas, alborotos y griteríos que, como era de esperarse, culminaron con mi visita a la oficina de la principal del Colegio San Vicente Ferrer. Sor Soledad recomendó la escritura en cursivas en la pizarra, de una sentencia amonestadora como castigo infalible y frente a todos: "Debo respetar la autoridad". Y yo así así lo hice. Escribí con tiza blanca en aquella plataforma verde, mis letras caligrafiadas a la perfección, mientras recitaba "la autoridad es mi abuela Petronila".

Nadie encadenado puede ser feliz. Por eso en el ejercicio de mi libertad, resucito a mi abuelamadre cada vez que me da la gana, cada vez que la sueño, cada vez que la alucino, cada vez que la escribo. Cada vez que ustedes leen *las Negras*.

Las negras que somos

ODETTE CASAMAYOR

¿QUIÉNES SOMOS, las mujeres negras de las Américas? ¿Quiénes han hecho posible nuestro presente existir? ¿Dónde encontrar nuestras madres? ¿Cómo recuperar su escondido legado, cuya existencia, sin embargo, nos es indiscutible? Porque, robustas, las sentimos a nuestras espaldas, depositando su aliento en nuestra voz; porque sabemos que a nuestras madres y abuelas y a sus madres y sus abuelas, multiplicadas en un innombrable contingente de mujeres secuestradas en África, desposeídas de su condición humana y trasplantadas como instrumentos de trabajo en las Américas, debemos nuestra supervivencia. Buscamos las madres desdibujadas tras páginas de historia escrita y cuidadosamente resguardada por quienes se esmeran en conservar el mismo orden, el mismo poder, atravesando siglos de recia colonialidad.

Por eso es "a los historiadores, por dejarnos fuera", a quienes Yolanda Arroyo Pizarro dedica Las negras, consciente de que los relatos de Wanwe, Ndizi, Tshanwe y Petra irrumpen para colmar vacíos históricos, deliberadamente ignorados. Desde los territorios de lo demoníaco, "demonic ground" certeramente identificados por Sylvia Wynter[1] como los espacios del imaginario de la exclusión al que somos relegadas las mujeres negras, avanzan las protagonistas a contar la silenciada experiencia esclava, ejerciendo la agencia que por siglos nos ha sido negada.

"Aquí estamos de nuevo... cuerpo presente", continúa anunciando la autora. Pues se sirve de la carne y el cuerpo para mejor reconstruir la borrosa narrativa de sus vidas. Los archivos históricos, rigurosamente recorridos para escribir Las negras, pueden haber aportado indicios de cómo pudo haber sido la existencia de estas mujeres, pero no serán nunca suficientes. No aparece en ellos la mujer negra más que "spectacularly violated, objectified, disposable, hypersexualized, and silenced,"[2] demostrando cómo la misma violencia exterminadora que arrasó con sus cuerpos mantiene amordazadas sus voces en los documentos a los que tradicionalmente se recurre para producir la historia.

Tan cimarrona como sus personajes, Yolanda Arroyo se insurge contra esta "violencia epistémica", que desborda los archivos y alcanza la comprensión generalizada de quienes fueron las mujeres esclavizadas y somos hoy sus descendientes. Si no contamos con datos fidedignos, si no ha sido registrada o no se ha prestado cabal atención a la agencia de las esclavas, si su testimonio fue posiblemente tergiversado para que se ajustaran a narrativas ajenas a las de aquellas mujeres, nos queda la carne, que se rebela y revela la indecible experiencia.

El camino de Yolanda es el mismo que hemos seguido muchas otras mujeres negras, en búsqueda de nuestros orígenes. Es aquel que en Lose your Mother tomaría Saidiya Hartman, decidida a recorrer "an itinerary of destruction from the coast to the savanna", excavando las heridas de nuestros ancestros esclavizados[3]. Una vez en Ghana, no pudo dejar de preguntarse si existiría realmente un lugar en el mundo capaz de saciar cuatrocientos años de nostalgia por identificar nuestro hogar[4]. No encontramos el hogar ni aquí ni allá: ni en las Américas o en Europa, donde nuestros cuerpos son doblegados por la alteridad y nuestra experiencia es estructuralmente silenciada; ni en África, donde los mismos cuerpos y la misma historia son también ignorados -por ausentes, olvidados y no apropiadamente memorializados. Elusivo hogar el nuestro que a veces imaginamos en mitad del océano, inalcanzable. "We have no ancestry except the black water and the Door of No Return," escribía Dionne Brand también intentando resolver el "dilema existencial" de los afrodescendientes.[5]

Las huellas de nuestro pasado parecen de tal suerte irrecuperables, pero conservamos la convicción de que no es así. En algún sitio nos esperan. "I think Blacks in the Diaspora carry the Door of No Return in our senses,"[6] se le volvió evidente a Dionne Brand; tanto como a Hartman que "We may have forgotten our country, but we haven't forgotten our dispossession."[7] Yolanda Arroyo Pizarro lo confirma cuando en Las negras nos propone un viaje similar. Sin embargo, la travesía no empuja lejos nuestros cuerpos, haciéndolos atravesar el Atlántico y confundirse en multitudes con las que, aun si compartimos colores y texturas, ni reconocemos ni nos reconocen completamente. Para reencontrarnos con nuestras antepasadas, la escritora no nos hace emprender el viaje físico. Solamente nos exhorta a habitar la carne de Wanwe, Ndizi, Tshanwe y Petra.

Así, la brutalidad de la Trata y los procesos de esclavizamiento son en su prosa pus y sangre manando de las heridas de estos personajes. Todo nos llega a través de las sensaciones en la carne de las cautivas. El pánico y la incertidumbre de la mujer africana que aún no comprende qué significarán su secuestro y transportación hacia inimaginables parajes, detrás de un océano hasta entonces desconocido, están volcados en su aturdimiento al escuchar el tumulto de idiomas incomprensibles, silencios y gemidos que en la bodega del barco al que ha sido lanzada se confunden con los suyos, mezclándose con la pestilencia y secreciones de aquel amasijo de carne del que ya es parte, sin saberlo. La conversión forzosa de la protagonista del primer cuento, Wanwe, es decir, la destrucción de su humanidad y fabricación de su identidad americana como mercancía, no es ese concepto nunca cabalmente aprehendido en incompletos intentos por explilcar la experiencia negra, utilizando metodologías académicamente legitimadas. Para Wanwe y para los lectores a quienes alcanza la palabra de Yolanda, el esclavizamiento no constituye un proceso abstracto, es vivencia. Ya en la carne de las protagonistas de los siguientes relatos, Ndizi, Tshanwe y Petra, en quienes la labor de esclavización ha sido completada, este proceso es expresado a través del dolor provocado por la tortura y la violación continuas.

Yolanda Arroyo Pizarro insiste en recordarnos que la historización de la experiencia afrodescendiente no debe iniciarse con el tradicional recuento del comercio trasatlántico de esclavizados. Los navíos en que fueron transportados a las Américas son con harta frecuencia elegidos como sitio simbólico del origen de la afrodescedencia. Pero, aunque una nueva no-vida, como bestias de carga, se impone a los africanos desde el momento mismo de su captura, su existencia y la de sus descendientes no comenzó durante la siniestra empresa esclavizadora.

Wanwe abre su cuento anunciando que su primer recuerdo podría ser el del barco al que la empujaron en África, pero pronto su mente viaja al pasado, deshaciendo el camino de su desposesión y volviendo mentalmente a la aldea de la infancia donde recupera, a pesar de las cadenas que en el momento del relato sellan su condición de esclava, su humanidad robada. A través de las memorias africanas de Wanwe, Tshanwe y Ndizi, concepciones del mundo diferentes a la que les fue impuesta son reconocidas, no sólo dentro del relato sino también en la historia de los afrodescendientes. Como muestran las heroínas de *Las negras,* nuestros ancestros trajeron consigo conocimientos inaccesibles a sus opresores, a los que echaron mano para resistir el aniquilamiento y la deshumanización. Si en África habían aprendido el arte de la curandería, en las Américas recurrirían a estos saberes para, a través del aborto y el infanticidio, evitar que los hijos de las esclavas tuvieran que padecer el mismo destino de sus madres a un tiempo que erosionaban el capital de los amos. Si guerreras y estrategas habían sido antes, una vez esclavizadas aprovecharían la arrogancia de los amos para escapar a la manigua y desde allí lanzarles saetas mortales. Conscientes eran del poder que en secreto aún detentaban: "El problema de los que oprimen, (. . .) no es la opresión en sí, es la subestimación que hacen del oprimido. (. . .) Ahora somos instigadas a no defendernos porque le pertenecemos a un amo. El opresor tiene ese permiso, pero nos subestima", advierte Ndizi al fraile que busca su confesión.

Yolanda Arroyo sabe que entre su carne y la de sus protagonistas se trenzan indestructibles hilos transgeneracionales. El dolor persiste, la opresión infligida también, a pesar de los siglos transcurridos entre la experiencia de nuestras antepasadas esclavizadas y la nuestra, como negras a quienes sistemáticamente se endilga la alteridad absoluta. Porque puede sentirla como propia, la escritora hace hábil uso de esa conexión para hilvanar la narrativa de la carne negra lacerada y doliendo. Carne también insurgente, pues no busca solamente *Las negras* devolvernos una recreación fenomenológica de la cruel desposesión de la humanidad en la mujer esclavizada.

En estas páginas, con más fuerza resuena el grito cimarrón que el del lamento. Las protagonistas se muestran inconformes con su condición de esclavas y, lo que es todavía más importante, con su condición de negras -como identidad construida por bajo la epistemología eurocéntrica. Las negras ya no son negras, porque solamente ellas pueden saber y decir quiénes realmente son. Poco importa que nunca desaparezcan de su piel las iniciales de los amos inscritas con hierro candente, no habrá modo de identificarlas si no lo hacen ellas. Y es entonces que dejan también de ser "las otras". En su autoconcepción no se conciben bajo las categorías fabricadas por sus opresores, sino a través de su propia identificación y visión del mundo.

Epistemologías distintas son pues esgrimidas por estas mujeres que son más que negras, porque se han dado luz a sí mismas. Socialmente muertas pueden ser consideradas desde la perspectiva de la sociedad que las aliena, pero ellas no se ven del todo inexistentes o indefensas. Viven en otro tiempo y espacio, por ellas forjados. Son los espacios de la manigua a la que escapan, al rebelarse real o figurativamente, y el recuerdo de la vida africana antes del secuestro, la travesía y el trasplante a las Américas. Confirman con ello que el cimarronaje no es apenas la mera fuga. La cimarrona es además procreadora de sí misma cuando, una vez que deshace sus cadenas, decide quién quiere ser y cómo actuar, dónde ser y qué pensar.

Mas regreso a las preguntas iniciales: ¿quiénes somos, las mujeres negras de las Américas? Silencio y monstruosidad comúnmente ensombrecen cada respuesta. Nos asaltan, por ejemplo, con sólo al recordar el torturado rostro de Anastácia.

No nos abandona, una vez que la hemos visto, esta imagen de la esclavizada rebelde condenada a portar un collar y una mordaza de hierro hasta su muerte. Aunque somos en realidad vistos por sus ojos, que nos fijan, manteniéndonos apresados por el indescifrable pero inescapable mensaje trasmitido por su mirada. La imagen de Anastácia amordazada golpea, transfiriendo su martirio a nuestra carne. Su historia, sin embargo, es incierta, como todas las historias de los africanos esclavizados y su descendencia. No tendremos jamás prueba de lo que verdaderamente sucedió con ella. No pudo expresarse, su boca en permanencia tapada con el bozal de hierro.

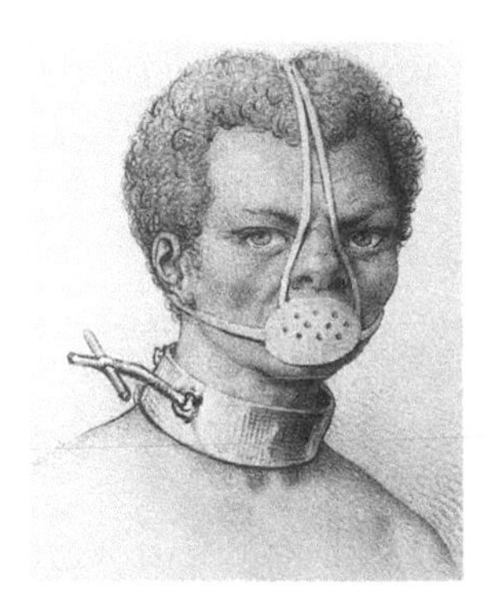

"Chatiment des Esclaves" (Brésil) 1838–1842

¡Ah, si Anastácia hubiera podido hablar!

Pero Yolanda Arroyo Pizarro recupera y recrea su voz en la historia de Wanwe, Ndizi, Tshanwe y Petra. Nadie va a decirnos quién fue Anastácia. Como tampoco ahora serán aquellos que producen la historia impuesta como universal, los que nos describen como monstruosas, criminales, consumidas por la furia, la lascivia, la inmoralidad, aquellos que definen nuestra presunta alteridad, quienes han de explicar cómo somos las mujeres negras. Solamente nosotras podemos relatarnos. Es pues necesario escuchar la voz de la mujer negra: todo el dolor y la rabia y el miedo y también la paz final. Paz guerrera. Paz insurgente. Paridora de mundos nuevos.

Notas

1 Wynter, Sylvia, "Afterword: Beyond Miranda's Meanings: Un/silencing the 'Demonic Ground' of Caliban's 'Woman.'" Boyce Davies, Carole and Elaine Savory Fido (eds.) *Out of the Kumbla: Caribbean Women and Literature*. Trenton: Africa World Press, 1990. 355-70.

2 Fuentes, Marisa J. *Dispossessed Lives: Enslaved Women, Violence, and the Archive*, Philadelphia: University of Pennsylvania Press, 2016. 5.

3 Hartman, Saidiya. *Lose Your Mother: A Journey Along the Atlantic Slave Route,* New York, Farrar, Straus & Giroux, 2007, 40.

4 Ibid., 33.

5 Brand, Dionne. *A Map to the Door of No Return. Notes to Belonging.* Toronto, Vintage Canada, 2001, 62.

6 Ibid., 48.

7 Hartman, 87.

EXORDIO A *LAS NEGRAS*

DRA. MARIE RAMOS ROSADO

EL TÍTULO del libro nos adelanta ya la temática de la diversidad, la cuestión de género y raza. *Las Negras* recoge cuatro textos narrativos: "Wanwe", "Matronas", "Saeta" y "Los amamantados". Las dedicatorias y citas a principio son reveladoras de las intenciones de la escritora. La autora dedica su libro a "los historiadores", y de inmediato aparece una cita del libro: Esclavos rebeldes. Conspiraciones y sublevaciones de esclavos en Puerto Rico, de Guillermo A. Baralt. La cita destaca la importancia que tuvieron los levantamientos de esclavos en el siglo XIX en Puerto Rico y la desinformación que existe entre la historia oficial con respecto a esas rebeliones, pues hubo gran secretismo y clandestinaje de estos movimientos, lo que nos hace pensar que la información histórica aún está incompleta. ¿Por qué ocurre esto? Está incompleta porque los(as) historiadores(as) han centrado sus investigaciones en las rebeliones realizadas por los esclavos y hombres negros, pero se han invisibilizado todas las gestiones realizadas por las mujeres negras. La historia puertorriqueña, como la universal, ha sido narrada desde una óptica patriarcal.

Por tanto, la dedicatoria del libro es una denuncia a la historia oficial: "por habernos dejado fuera." Se está reclamando la visibilidad histórica de las mujeres esclavas. Tal parece que la escritora decide, a través de la ficción, hacer visible a todas las mujeres negras y destacar las aportaciones que han realizado a la humanidad, pues aún no parecen ser reconocidas. La autora logra su objetivo mediante un cuarteto de textos: "Wanwe", "Matronas", "Saeta" y "Los amamantados".

En estas narraciones, Yolanda Arroyo Pizarro destaca la valentía y firmeza de las mujeres negras, quienes "tomaron partido en las miles de fugas individuales y grupales en las épocas esclavistas" (Soyna 15). También de sus narraciones se infieren los roles activos y protagónicos que tuvieron estas negras en la mayoría de las revueltas y sediciones. Sin embargo, permanecen invisibilizadas en la historia oficial y canónica.

Este libro aporta a la valoración y reconocimiento de los trabajos ejercidos por las mujeres negras esclavas en América: comadronas, curanderas, yerberas, sobadoras, nodrizas, santiguadoras, cuenteras, sirvientas, cocineras, ordeñadoras de vacas, etc. Además visibiliza las luchas de resistencia de estas heroínas negras en papeles protagónicos.

las Negras & Yo, Makandal

Ay, ay, ay, que soy grifa y pura negra;
grifería en mi pelo
cafrería en mis labios;
y mi chata nariz mozambiqueña.

—Julia de Burgos
Ay, ay, ay de la grifa negra

porque nací mujer y sangro y me preñan y paro
y crío y cuido y limpio y organizo y dejo de sangrar.

—Johanny Vázquez Paz
Poemas Callejeros / Streetwise Poems

A los historiadores, por habernos dejado fuera.

———

Aquí estamos de nuevo...
cuerpo presente, color vigente,
declinándonos a ser invisibles...
rehusándonos a ser borradas.

———

A mi Aurora Eterna

———

A mis profesores Raúl Guadalupe, Josué Santiago
y Miguel Rodríguez López

———

las Negras

Relatos

Hasta fecha muy reciente, solamente se tenía conocimiento de un muy reducido número de conspiraciones y sublevaciones de esclavos ocurridas durante el pasado siglo XIX. Sin embargo, esta investigación basada principalmente en las fuentes primarias documentales de varios municipios de Puerto Rico, demuestra que, contrario a lo que siempre se había creído, los esclavos de la isla se rebelaron con frecuencia. El número de conspiraciones conocidas para apoderarse de los pueblos y de la isla, más los incidentes para asesinar a los blancos, y particularmente a los mayordomos, sobrepasa los cuarenta intentos. Mas, si tomamos en consideración la secretividad y el clandestinaje de estos movimientos, el número resultaría, indiscutiblemente, muy superior.

—Guillermo A. Baralt
Esclavos rebeldes. Conspiraciones y sublevaciones de esclavos en Puerto Rico (1795–1873)

Las mujeres negras tomaron partido en las miles de fugas individuales y grupales que se desataron en épocas esclavistas y subsiguientes, de este lado del orbe. Jugaron roles activos y protagónicos en la mayoría de las sediciones y revueltas celebradas, en pura manifestación de rebeldía. Cansadas como estaban de la institución de la esclavitud y todo tipo de otras restricciones a la libertad, transgredieron, infringieron y quebrantaron el orden.

—Gabriela Sonya

He conocido mujeres valientes que explotaron los límites de la posibilidad humana, sin ninguna historia que las guiara.

—Gloria Steinem

I get angry about things, then go on and work.

—Toni Morrison

Wanwe

1.

El primer recuerdo pudiera ser el barco. Una barriga de maderos unidos y flotantes a quienes los suyos llaman *owba coocoo*. Tanta enormidad, tanto espacio. Un conglomerado de leños apretados, vigas y tablones labrados y unidos con algún desconocido procedimiento. Palos anchos repujados y de feo color. Varios poseen un musgo adherido, aquellos cercanos al agua. Nunca antes vistos por Wanwe.

La llevan al barco, en una canoa pequeña, en compañía de otras mujeres. Van atadas.

Una de las mujeres tiene orejeras y un pendiente de nariz. No es de la casta de Wanwe y ni siquiera habla su idioma. Sin que nadie lo note, de manera silenciosa, desamarra con astucia las sogas de sus extremidades y, acto seguido, se lanza de la canoa. Dos hombres se arrojan al agua tras ella. Logran alcanzarla, la agarran del torso y la golpean. El chapoteo del mar da cuenta de la violenta golpiza. Wanwe nota que la espuma blanca, en ocasiones, se vuelve roja. La devuelven a la canoa, atándola esta vez del cuello e inmovilizan sus manos detrás de su espalda. Le halan el cabello y desgarran los aretes de ambos lóbulos de oreja. Esperan a que pare de llorar y desgarran el del tabique. Es poco lo que comprende Wanwe o las demás mujeres que miran, pero perciben que se trata de un acto de control. Los hombres imparten más fuerza en el amarre del cuello y la mujer tose, pero además lanza patadas.

Las otras mujeres sentadas dan alaridos. Wanwe cierra los llorosos ojos y los demás captores realizan ademanes, unas amenazas con movimientos sin ritmo, para que se calmen. Les muestran puñales, gesticulaciones de maldad en cejas y mejillas amarillentas y la lengua que sacan y recogen, a medida que abren y cierran la boca, llena de griteríos apestosos a algún tipo de estiércol con licor.

Las venas de alrededor del cogote de la mujer que ha intentado escaparse se tensan, parecen explotar, entonces ella babea. Siguen apretándola hasta que se desmaya, o su espíritu va a encontrarse con los bailadores poderosos de las puertas del inframundo. Wanwe quisiera tener la certeza de ese paso de portal hacia las esencias ancestrales, quisiera poder realizar alguna plegaria que diera luz al ánima encarnada hasta el ánima desmaterializada.

Quisiera pintar la frente, cortar con marcas de hierro la piel de los hombros para marcar a esa mujer hermana en su pasaje. Pero no puede. Está imposibilitada para realizar nada a favor de esa alma.

Uno de los hombres hamaquea la soga al otro extremo y la exhibe, como escarmiento a las otras.

2.

Previo a ese momento, Wanwe ha visto el mar, únicamente, otras dos veces.

Llegar hasta él, desde su hogar, toma siete días de trayecto. Hay que cruzar una vasta región, dormir a la intemperie, pegadita de los hombros de las demás jovencitas que aún no sangran y danzar en el rito del *ureoré*. Cuando llega de visita a la aldea lejana, en donde se ve el mar, las ancianas le enseñan, como secretos de bienvenida, la confección de pócimas para la guerra.

Wanwe cierra los ojos y recuerda el aroma de las viejas, de su madre, de las hermanas, de las muchachas en el rito del ureoré. Cualquier cosa que le haga olvidar, en este preciso momento, que la mujer de los aretes arrancados apenas respira.

3.

La suben al barco grande, a ella y a las otras. Mientras camina por cubierta, Wanwe descubre vigas altas con inmensas telas colgantes y amarres de un material muy distinto al utilizado en la aldea. Listones color crema opaco, con nudos en diferentes partes de una misma soga que parecen suspendidos por los aires. El suelo es duro, con astillas que a veces se incrustan en los dedos y en las plantas de los pies. Y hay pestes, muy malos olores por derredor.

Wanwe mira sus manos sujetadas, como si fuera la primera vez que nota que de su cuerpo brotan extremidades indefensas, pero lo cierto es que lleva horas observándose. Se siente extraña, como salida de su propio cuerpo. Observa los acontecimientos aún sin entender del todo.

Supone que lo mismo les sucede a las dos mujeres que ahora caminan por cubierta antes que ella, en fila. Hasta imagina que las tres de atrás cavilan sobre la misma situación. Puede ver pocas cosas desde ese ángulo. No sabe cuántas son en total, pero sí sabe que todas son mujeres.

Por alguna razón, durante el camino del traslado desde la aldea hasta la playa, ha sido lastimada en el ojo derecho. El ojo duele mucho y le supura. Nota que hay barandas desde donde se puede extrañar la costa, oler el mar, probar los chasquidos de ola.

4.

La costa se hace cada vez más chica, más distante. La mujer que camina justo frente a ella, que tiene la frente marcada, sigue gravemente enferma. Esa marca la identifica como perteneciente a una etnia del sur. Vomita de cada dos o tres pasos y las demás se esfuerzan por mantenerla en marcha. A pesar de la situación en que se encuentran, algunas van entonando un cántico. Otras deslizan por los labios partidos apenas un murmullo repetido, como aquellos que aprendieron en el rezo de las mañanas y en las lamentaciones fúnebres. Cuando ocurre la muerte de un jefe, o de una madre de territorio—aquellas llamadas así debido a que poseen multitud de hijos—sus familiares y allegados se reúnen a la cabecera de su lecho y gritan la pena de su fallecimiento. Algunos se dan a la tarea de colocar su cadáver boca abajo y cubrirlo con una manta. Acto seguido, se lanzan a las calles, con ramas de árboles en las manos, para hacer pública la noticia mediante los cantos funerales. Gritan exclamaciones corales que se acompañan de gran dolor: *epá, baba wa loni. iyu li a nwa ko ri, mo de oja, ko si loju, mo de ita, ko si ni ita, mo de ile, ko si ni ile, ngko ni ri o, o da gbere, o di arinako.*

Wanwe desearía escalar un árbol, hacerse de una rama larga y agitarla para marcar el despacho de la mujer sofocada y su cuerpo desprendido o a punto de desprenderse. Pero no puede e intuye que, a partir de ahora, jamás volverá a hacerlo.

5.

El primer recuerdo también pudiera ser la aldea. El correteo de los chicos y las chicas, el juego de los hombros.

En el rito del *ureoré*, las niñas que se han criado unidas, como hermanas, duermen una pegadita a la otra, formando una hilera que une a cada cual por el área de los hombros. Cuando los mayores no están mirando y logran encontrar un pastizal alto que les cubre hasta la cabeza, las niñas juegan al *ureoré* con los varones. Si los adultos los encuentran, irían todos al castigo, porque el juego de hombros es un juego de féminas, prohibido a los machos.

Primero los colocan de pie, al lado de ellas y se les pegan, brazo con brazo. Usualmente se unen a algún chico que les gusta. La cercanía sirve para dejarles saber cuál de ellos huele bien, cuán suave se siente la piel, rozando juntos, cómo se acoplan los latidos de corazón, porque ambos lo sienten como un tamborileo.

Los juegos del *ureoré* clandestino lo hacen a escondidas, no sólo de los adultos, sino también de los más pequeñitos, aquellos que sin querer pudieran indiscretamente enterar a los mayores. Es sabido que el gesto de hombro con hombro es un preámbulo serio al ritual de casamiento. Solo las niñas que han sido dadas en compromiso deben tocarse de esa manera con los varones escogidos.

En la etnia de Wanwe, la niña escoge al varón con el que va a casarse. La madre ayuda en la selección y da consejo. El padre prepara la festividad de la promesa junto al padre y la madre del varón elegido. Una madre puede decirle a su hija que se fije en los ojos del muchacho, o en sus labios gruesos, en la nariz grande y los brazos fornidos. Los jovencitos que saben nadar, cazar y tocar las tamboras con mayor habilidad serán los recomendados. Una niña que ya ha tenido su primera sangre, tiene hasta su ciclo veintinueve para elegir.

6.

Wanwe recuerda el día del compromiso de su hermana Bosuá. Sacrifican un jabalí y todos comen y beben durante la ceremonia. Trae a su memoria las espigas de su tierra Namib y a sus dunas de arena que tantas veces sirven de escondite a ella y a los parientes en los juegos de aldea. Recuerda los sonidos de chasquido de lenguas, tan peculiares del idioma de su localidad. Recuerda con nostalgia cómo celebran la llegada de los recién nacidos confeccionando golosinas del fruto de las palmeras. Recuerda las piernas largas de sus hermanas. Cómo las alzan y bajan, rodillas dobladas, extremidades estiradas, dando alaridos en trance, en medio del baile.

Wanwe no puede olvidar el rostro de felicidad de Bosuá, ni cómo se miran los prometidos, ni cómo, cuando nadie observa, se unen de los hombros y hacen temblar las pieles. El secreto que comparten Bosuá y Wanwe, y que nadie más sabe, es que juntas ellas ya han escogido con anterioridad al joven Semö desde que todos eran más jovencitos. Con frecuencia han jugado aquel juego prohibido.

7.

El problema en sí no es el juego, ni la cercanía de los hombros. Wanwe sabe que el verdadero dilema es la cercanía de las sienes y las mejillas . . . porque a veces, si se descubre un nerviosismo de piernas—planta del pie que tropieza, rodilla que se dobla, pantorrillas que ceden al acercamiento—el estremecimiento de vientres embarrados del lodo del río es tan poderoso, que en ocasiones las niñas han accedido a frotarse con los niños frente con frente, un labio con otro.

8.

Es posible que el primer recuerdo también sea el día del secuestro.

Nadie sabía que les atraparían.

Así pues, salen varias madres de cacería, sin sospechar nada, llevando a sus críos a la espalda. Lo único que se necesita es una pieza de tela resistente y mucha hambre. Con un simple movimiento del trapo, la madre se inclina hacia adelante, coloca al bebé sobre la columna de sus vértebras y lo sujeta contra su cuerpo pasando el paño alrededor de ambos y anudándolo. Las hermanitas y hermanitos mayores, aquellos que ya caminan, llevan consigo las hachas y navajas, colocadas de un modo seguro en sus bolsos. Esperan a que las madres silben, como clave inequívoca de que se acerca una presa. Si el silbido es corto, breve, el animal atisbado es pequeño. Entonces, los demás hijos se emocionan porque saben que pueden tomar partido de la caza. Si el silbido es alargado, extenso, los chicos corren a esconderse, no sin antes entregar las armas a la progenitora.

Wanwe recuerda haber visto que se les envuelven los bracitos a los recién nacidos con la banda, aunque a los niños más crecidos les gusta tener los brazos libres. Casi nunca se cae un niño mientras su madre se lo ata a la espalda o se va de cacería con los demás hijos. A veces los pequeños lloran porque no quieren estar ahí, o se atemorizan si el animal identificado es demasiado feroz y hace ruidos intimidantes. Pero la madre sujeta bien los bracitos presionándoselos debajo de los suyos, canta alguna tonada tranquilizadora y con movimientos certeros y expertos, deja sin vida a la presa en pocos minutos.

Esa tarde, a pesar de las lluvias y los ríos salidos de cauce, las madres de la aldea se pintan los rostros de amarillo y logran acumular caza para varios días. Algunas logran atrapar peces con las pértigas, gracias a la crecida de las aguas confluentes.

Ya están a punto de regresar, cuando la madre de Wanwe y Bosuá se detiene, impartiendo la orden de alerta. Tanto ella como algunas otras detectan la presencia de otro animal posiblemente grande y peligroso. Un animal, o varios, que no temen; en vez de alejarse, se acercan. Las tupidas gotas de lluvia dificultan la tarea de discernimiento auditivo.

Wanwe y Bosuá echan a correr tan pronto el silbido prolongado de la madre se hace sentir.

El pitido se alarga como una liana de árbol gigante, interminable. Como un helecho adornado de musgos rizomatosos, sin principio ni fin.

Corren ahora los demás chicos, las otras madres, las ráfagas de lluvia y dardos que empiezan a atiborrar la selva, pasándoles por el lado, encajándose algunos en la piel. Corren los relámpagos, las lanzas, las macanas impulsadas con fuerza que empiezan a caer sobre las espaldas y los cráneos de quienes escapan.

El sonido de la voz de la madre—ahora lejana—se estira, se funde, se confunde con otros ruidos, las alertas, los peligros, el dolor, la sangre, el cuerpo caído. Los cuerpos magullados. Las manos encadenadas.

Las presas atrapadas para la cena se caen, ruedan por la hierba, por los arbustos con troncos sin ramificar o raramente ramificados y son arrastradas por las lluvias torrentosas del suelo. Los animales muertos ya han dejado de ser parte del botín, ya no son cena; acaso se convierten en carroña abandonada que seguramente será devorada por alguna otra bestia.

9.

Wanwe es atrapada por el pie. Tropieza y cae. No puede ver a su hermana, no sabe de ella. Ha perdido de vista a su madre silbadora y a los otros hermanos.

En los largos segundos en que su rostro viaja desde la distancia conocida de pie, hasta la que permite la gravedad tumbarla, mientras su cráneo toca el suelo y lacera su ojo, no deja de escuchar, en ningún momento, el silbido. Voltea la cabeza, buscando. Buscándola. El silbido que se sigue extendiendo, que sigue advirtiendo, que continúa alertando a los otros sobre aquella calamidad enorme, se ahoga de pronto ante la certeza de que hay que fugarse. Correr lejos. Alejarse del enemigo.

Pero nada de ello sucede.

Una maldición se ha ensañado sobre ellos. Un griterío identificado desde otras gargantas. Órdenes de atrapar, enjaular, llevar a los barcos y canjear sus existencias entre los visitantes de la costa.

10.

Para cuando Wanwe vuelve a pensar en su madre, en el juego de los hombros, en Bosúa y su joven novio, en sus hermanos, en las lianas de burkeas, las raíces de ceiba, en las cebras, los jabalíes y los babuinos, ya los vecinos del Imperio del este la tienen amarrada y la transportan a la orilla. Una orilla que previo a ese momento Wanwe solamente ha visto otras dos veces. Llegar hasta el mar, desde su hogar, toma siete días de trayecto. Hay que cruzar una vasta región, distinguir el relieve bastante uniforme de la costa, encontrar la playa formada por extensas mesetas de arena y dormir a la intemperie

11.

Durante los cantares de aldea que dirigen los jefes y ancianos, Wanwe recuerda escuchar las antiguas leyendas; aquellas que cuentan que mirando a la Luna puede una fácilmente ver una rana. Una rana que no salta, que se mantiene estática y gira, según gire la eterna esfera compañera del planeta.

Las madres de territorio cuentan a todos sus hijos que la rana es un animal lunar, portadora de agua, de lluvias, tormentas y lágrimas. Es testigo de injusticias, especialmente las que se cometen entre hermanos de etnia.

Wanwe sospecha que aquel animal lunar, que pertenece al elemento húmedo del universo y que brilla junto a las estrellas aparentemente encadenadas en el oscuro cielo, no es culpable de los secuestros. Cree que no son las aguas de la Luna las responsables de que la mujer que tiene la frente marcada y que ya no camina frente a ella—las mantienen ahora a todas de pie, en fila, como si esperaran un turno para algo desconocido—continúe vomitando sollozos, o sollozando vómitos.

Balbucea Wanwe, para despistarse de tanto dolor, que el anfibio que habita en la Luna tiene tres patas y que sus tres patas simbolizan las fases lunares.

12.

Las colocan acostadas, unas cerquita de otras, en el sótano del barco. Tan pegaditas como si fueran a jugar el ureoré. Wanwe mira a sus dos compañeras de hombros, una a la derecha y otra a la izquierda. Todas respiran con el mismo espanto y vacilación.

Entran hombres a aquel lugar tan oscuro y tan encajonado en la parte inferior de la barcaza, con órdenes de marcar con fuego a todas las cautivas. Usan unas letras de hierro caliente, con las iniciales de quienes de seguro pasarán a ser sus nuevos dueños.

13.

Los seres ancestrales no las liberan. No hacen acto de presencia, a pesar de haber sido convocados con todas las fuerzas. Tampoco asoman las nuevas deidades que adoran los chamanes de sus captores, aquellos que visten sotanas, usan un emblema en cruz y lanzan un líquido bendecido con rezos.

No hacen acto de presencia Orún, Olódùmarè, Bàbá, Ìyá ni las diosas que aún están en la Tierra, ni los verbos conjugados desde el cielo, ni los sabios del mar, ni las esencias ancestrales de culto.

Olórun desaparece.

Oníbodè desaparece.

Ìbí, Ìyé, Áti, Ikú desaparecen.

No se vislumbra el espíritu de los rituales de río, ni el paso por la compuerta del Portero, ni la pintura de rojo para la danza. No más nacimiento, vida y muerte.

Los miedos de todas ellas, hermanas, se reducen a esto: ¿Quién diseñará nuestro posible retorno? ¿Quién nos abrazará en el Àtúnwa si hemos sufrido tanto? ¿Cuándo volveremos a ser libres para el *ureoré*?

14.

El capitán de la nao amarra las piernas a la mujer que había intentado escapar en la orilla, durante el trayecto de las canoas. Respira poco. Sus desangradas orejas y orificios nasales no le permiten gritar. Se retuerce, lucha, pero lo hace con un llanto silencioso mientras es levantada en vilo, desde el suelo, por los pies.

Cabeza abajo y amarrada también de las manos, varios hombres colaboran para lanzarla al mar.

Wanwe y las otras observan la escena intentando identificarla. ¿Será de las cazadoras amarillas del norte, de las costureras azules del sur? ¿Acaso las bailarinas rojas del oeste? ¿Cuántos hijos tendrá, cuántas veces habrá jugado? ¿Habrá usado máscaras en las guerras contra los imperios o en las reyertas de aldea?

La escena muta. El capitán arroja al mar a una mujer que ahora sí grita con pánico. De repente Wanwe hace contacto visual con ella, ojos míos con ojos suyos, justo antes de verla hundirse. El océano se la traga.

Wanwe piensa que va a ahogarse, pero el poco tiempo que pasa sumergida le basta para saber que aquel final para ella no es posible. En vez de ese, será otro.

Cuando momentos después vuelven a alzarla y ella es levantada por los pies como una guerrera de alabastro que parece inmortalizarse, su cuerpo ya ha sido partido a la mitad por los mordiscos de varios tiburones.

15.

Por primera vez desde que Wanwe deja la selva, vuelve a oír el silbido. Una sirena de alarma que anuncia peligro. El sonido de aquella boca es inconfundible; pitido que se alarga como una liana de árbol gigante, interminable. Un hueco que se escucha y se siente. No sabe desde qué parte del barco se origina o hacia dónde va. No sabe si es al norte, sur, este u oeste, mar adentro, mar afuera, brisa, viento, proa, eslora, popa. Lo que sí conoce es que aquella caricia de tímpano es suficiente excusa para gritar asfixiada y llorosa el nombre de mamá.

My home now seemed more dreary than ever. The laugh of the little slave-children sounded harsh and cruel. It was selfish to feel so about the joy of others. My brother moved about with a very grave face. I tried to comfort him, by saying, "Take courage, Willie; brighter days will come by and by."

Incidents in the Life of a Slave Girl

—Harriet Ann Jacobs

Matronas

1.

El hombre recién ingresado al calabozo viene vestido de monje. Pienso en la posibilidad de que sea un fraile católico. También puede ser un sacerdote o un aspirante, de esos denominados seminaristas. Los blancos, a los aspirantes, le dicen por un nombre que ahora no recuerdo. Son tantas las palabras que no recuerdo ya. A veces me molesta darme cuenta de que desconozco totalmente la frase para llamar a las jirafas. Cuando entro en el pánico de lo que he olvidado, inicio un recuento mental: pedirle a mi madre que me abrace, gritar por comida, convocar a las hermanas, bromear con los infantes. Esas frases las recuerdo perfectamente en mi idioma. Hay otras que llegan a mi mente en otras lenguas, dependiendo de cuánto tiempo haya pasado en algunas plantaciones rodeada de gente de otras castas. También recuerdo palabras en castellano: las nanas cantadas a los hijos de los amos, las recetas aprendidas en el puerto español, las especias del mercado, la confección de carnes, las oraciones de los santísimos cristianos. Además, sé un poco de la lengua de los nativos, aquellos que los blancos llaman taínos y que escasean. Y si me concentro lo suficiente, mientras purgo el castigo de los once días encerrada en esta cárcel, en medio de esta soledad, puedo recitar algo así como un himno entonado por los holandeses, un tipo de cántico en el que desprecian a la tierra denominada Francia.

Pero ahora, ya no estoy sola. Han entrado a la mazmorra el capataz y el sereno, acompañados del hombre vestido con túnica. Una sola vez usé un atuendo de vestir igual a ése, mientras intentaba escapar con un grupo de mandingos. Los negros mandingos salieron del mar una tarde mientras me encontraba haciendo trabajos en la playa, camino al trapiche Segovia. Eran negros fugados que se habían lanzado de la embarcación antes de esta atracar en puerto. Nadie los había visto, o al menos, nadie aún los buscaba. Me cubrieron con una sotana mojada que les sobraba y me uní a ellos. Eran tres hombres y una mujer, malnutridos y deshidratados. Los dirigí a robar alimentos y continué a su lado por voluntad propia, a pesar de que al quinto día los hombres se amancebaron conmigo, sin yo consentirlo. La mujer miró hacia otro lado, temblorosa. Luego se acostaron con ella también. No soy de la casta de los mandingos, pero cierto tipo de lealtad me hizo no dejarles y fungí como traductora, ya que algunos no entendían el idioma de los amos. Aunque no soy ladina, lo entiendo a la perfección. Lo entiendo pero lo guardo como secreto.

2.

El hombre monje es blanco, pero diferente. Creo descubrir una mirada de sorpresa y compasión en sus ojos rosados, si es que eso existe entre los conquistadores. Incluso entre sacerdotes y monjas, nunca identifico sentimiento alguno de solidaridad. Este hombre es distinto. Tiene algo distinto.

¿Hablas castellano?, pregunta y me le quedo mirando esa primera vez. Finjo que no he comprendido y el capataz me pega en el rostro alegando que sí sé. Me exige que conteste, pero me quedo observando al monje en silencio. Se toca el pecho y dice Petro. Yo hago lo mismo y contesto Ndizi. Él lo repite, pronunciando tres silabas por separado de modo profusamente nasal. Digo que sí con la cabeza.

Acto seguido, Petro inicia un recital de dialectos zonificados, intentando suertes: kimbundu, mandingo, bantú, francés, holandés, creoles derivados de éstos. Debo tener cuidado con este hombre, anoto en mi cabeza. Debo recordar no contarle jamás todo lo que sé, lo que he visto, lo que he sentido. Decido contestarle en la lengua de los yoruba y él sonríe. Como mejor puede, me dice en ese idioma: prometo practicar más el yoruba para regresar a hablar en unos días contigo. Sin querer, yo también sonrío. El capataz y el sereno no parecen contentarse.

Un rato más tarde, Petro se despide y se marcha. Lo observo caminar mientras sale de mi celda. Cruza la puerta que da camino hacia afuera, hacia la libertad, de donde yo no soy. Antes era mía. Antes, en mi natal aldea, donde jugaba con la manada de cebras y mis abuelas, que eran varias, me enseñaban a confeccionar pócimas. Cuando pienso en libertad siempre pienso en todas las palabras de todos los lenguajes que conozco, en donde esta expresión quiere decir algo. Y me sucede como con la palabra pereza o descanso; no recuerdo su significado en todos los idiomas que me sé. Tampoco sé cómo se dice látigo en wolof, aunque pueda pronunciarlo en congolés. Entonces el capataz y el sereno vuelven a golpearme, a amarrarme y a penetrarme con sus penes rancios.

3.

La segunda vez que Petro nos visita (y digo nos, porque ahora tengo más compañía: han encarcelado junto a mí a una nueva comadrona), llega con un libro que en principio presiento es la biblia. Luego me doy cuenta de que no lo es. Son una serie de papeles en los que ha escrito algunas frases en yoruba. Me las lee y le contesto. Pausadamente. Imitando el desconocimiento que demuestran los novicios de una lengua. Me pregunta la edad y le digo que, según el conteo de las tribus del norte, tengo treintitantos años. Pero aclaro, en imperfecto español, que fui apresada por el imperio de los negros de la costa y vendida a los blancos hace más de quince. Hecha cocinera, obrera de la caña y comadrona hace más de diez. ¿Qué cocinas?, pregunta él en cristiano y le refuto, ahora en lengua esclava, lo primero que se me viene a la mente: algo que tiene que ver con la cocción de cerdos degollados, mollejas, rabos y orejas de animal. Le cuento cualquier cosa, con pocos detalles, pero en realidad sé cocinar todo lo que me pongan de frente y de modo exquisito. Puedo incluso confeccionar veneno de lenta interacción, aderezado con guarapo y canela.

Petro enuncia algunos fonemas espaciados, otros más fluidos. Construye frases con la conjunción de una palabra que parece ser *mtoto, /m. to.to/ child / petit nené*, o algo parecido. Asiento con la cabeza y él me mira largo rato. Me mira queriendo saber si es cierto de lo que se me acusa. La comadrona a mi lado llora y él se confunde. Piensa que llora por los niños muertos.

4.

Rememoro, entre dormida y despierta, las fogatas realizadas durante el escape con los yorubas. Encendemos piras con residuos de madera y palmeras porque hace frío de noche y es demasiado oscuro. Logramos acceso a varias cuevas hasta sentirnos seguros de haber dejado atrás a nuestros perseguidores. En ellas colocamos antorchas, descansamos y esbozamos un plan para regresarnos al continente. Luego de varias horas de argumentos nos damos por vencidos. No va a suceder. Necesitaríamos recursos, barcazas, armas, suministros para el viaje de vuelta y otros menesteres que no poseemos. Concluimos que lo mejor es morir, antes que humillarnos al opresor y hablamos de algunos hermanos nuestros, expertos en la práctica del suicidio compasivo, que ya lo han logrado y que han dejado instrucciones como legado. Menciono el caso de Undraá, forzada a cohabitar con todos los hombres blancos de la nao en la que viajamos desde el continente hasta esta isla, mujer conocedora del mar y sus especies por vivir tantos años siendo parte del grupo de pescadoras amarillas. Esperó estar en altamar, cerca de los nidos de tiburones. Se lanzó a las aguas. Los yorubas mencionan otros hermanos. Bguiano, experto colmillero de la localidad sahariana, perteneciente a un ejército de hombres que afilaba continuamente sus dientes y mataba a las bestias selváticas con lucha cuerpo a cuerpo y mordidas. Bguiano se hizo de un grupo de bozales en la plantación en la que servía y les ensenó su habilidad.

Luego prestaron juramento ante changó y a todo aquel que lo deseaba, le extirpaban de una sola mordedura, la vena más visiblemente palpitadora del cuello. Recordamos a Zeza, brebajero y confeccionador de hechizos, que sabía la combinación exacta de cada hierba de región venenosa para hacer cerrar los ojos y nunca más volver a abrirlos. Así fuimos, poco a poco mencionando ideas y algunos quedándose dormidos.

Yo bostezo y hago juramento, por las deidades de los vientos de las que dudo ya, que si soy capturada nuevamente, me las habré de cobrar con los niños.

5.

Petro me da toquecitos en el rostro para que despierte. Su rosada y familiar mirada me da de beber. Deposita en mi garganta agua y una medicina hecha de plantas analgésicas para aminorar los dolores de cuerpo. Hablabas en sueños, dice, y cuando se acerca el carcelero disimula murmurando las cuentas del rosario en latín. Luego usa pedazos de sílabas compuestas para explicarme que no soy una bestia. *Mbwa / m.bwa/ perro*; *tembo /elefant/thembo/elephant*; *ne.nda/ not / no; tú/toi*. Hay una rebelde empatía en su tono que me hace creerle y hasta sentir lástima por él. Murmuro en francés y se queda de una pieza ante el descubrimiento de mi dominio lingüista. Lo repito en castellano y en igbo. Petro me tapa la boca con su mano para que guarde silencio y no me descubran. Se acercan celadores. Dan de comer sobras de las hacien das aledañas a las otras dos mujeres que me acompañan en la celda, pero nada a mí. He sido declarada Negra Sediciosa e Insurrecta en los tablones públicos, identificada por mi lunar cerca del ojo, el carimbo en forma de "P" en mi frente y la oferta de recompensa por mi captura. Cuando se van, Petro extrae casabe que lleva escondido y me lo coloca en la boca, invitándome a que lo mastique poco a poco, no vaya a ahogarme. Las otras mujeres comparten su agua conmigo. Todo me sabe a las golosinas que se confeccionan en el valle de nuestro río de origen, durante la ceremonia de máscaras.

Entre ruidos fricativos, guturales, chasquidos parecidos a los lamentos musicales de los tribales cuando son atrapados, posesivos aspirados, tartamudeos, consonantes cortas, vocales largas, plurales y singulares con y sin apóstrofes, Petro me asegura que guardará el secreto. Lo único que quiere es saber, documentar esta violencia que se ha desatado en la humanidad, explica, esta histórica bestialidad. Hay frailes en las otras islas escribiendo crónicas sobre los eventos; yo quiero narrar este. Nos hacemos pasar por colaboradores de la corona, pero no es así. Juro que no voy a traerte líos.

¿Lo juras por tu dios?, le increpo, y cuando dice que sí, lo amonesto: Pero tu dios no tiene poder ni fuerza alguna, es indolente, débil, sin propósito. ¿Cómo permite esto? Petro asiente. Baja la cabeza en lo que únicamente puedo percibir como un gesto de vergüenza. Me pregunta en qué deidades creo yo y cuestiona si en ayé, oyá, obatalá. En ninguna, le digo y se me saltan las lágrimas. Todas nos abandonaron.

6.

Os juro que quise morir, Fray Petro, a ser usada como animal. Os juro que luego quise matar a todos, padrecito. Nous allons reproduire une armée, kite a kwaze yon lame. Eso me propuse. Eso nos propusimos las mujeres y corrimos la voz en los toques de tambores. Hebu kuzaliana jeshi. Repetimos lo mismo en los festines de música wolof, tuareg, bakongos, malimbo y los egba. Las noticias siguieron corriendo en cantatas a los balimbe, ovimbundu y el resto. Todas las que somos del Congo, y las que somos de Ibibio y las que somos de Seke o de Cabindala respondimos. Let us breed an army. Forgemos un ejército.

El problema de los que oprimen, Fray Petro, no es la opresión en sí; es la subestimación que hacen del oprimido. Siempre presto atención al rostro de vitalidad o cansancio de aquellos que entran al cuerpo de una mujer sin su permiso. En mi aldea, si algo así llegaba a suceder, los transgresores eran castigados y se les cobraba una infracción según los bienes que poseían. Si un hombre ultrajaba a una mujer joven o madura, casada o sin marido, debía pagar con sus posesiones, y si no tenía ninguna, responder con la extirpación a sangre fría de algún órgano expuesto de su cuerpo; un brazo, una mano, un pie, alguna oreja, hasta la nariz.

Las mujeres éramos animadas a defendernos, a golpear, morder, arrancar. Las cosas han cambiado desde que los negros iniciaron secuestros hacia otros negros y nos entregaron a los portugueses u otros blancos, para transportarnos en nao. Ahora somos instigadas a no defendernos porque le pertenecemos a un amo. El opresor tiene ese permiso, pero nos subestima.

Siempre presto atención al rostro de vitalidad o cansancio de aquellos que entran al cuerpo de una mujer sin su permiso, Fray Petro. Así me topé ante el rostro invadido de éxtasis del sereno de la otra cárcel, una tarde en que acababa de forzarme. No respetó siquiera que la sangre de ochún se me estaba resbalando por los muslos de mis días lunares. Cerró los ojos por un segundo, vaciado. Segundo que bastó para darme cuenta de que estaba solo... que me tomaría poco esfuerzo.

Echó la cabeza hacia atrás en un gesto de arrobamiento por su eyaculación y se distrajo. Lo mordí. Llevé mis dientes hasta su glande y apreté virulenta, como los cerdos rabiosos. En principio intentó dar un golpe. Acto seguido cayó desorientado y herido, con gran dolor. Mientras se agarraba desequilibrado y gimiente en el suelo, retiré las llaves de la reja de su pantalón, abrí el cerrojo, volví a cerrarlo y fui una por una por el resto de las celdas. Liberé a ladinos, cimarrones y nativos. Y a las comadronas que vienen luchando conmigo.

7.

Curandera, yerbera, sobadora, comadrona. He desempeñado todas las faenas de una esclava doméstica para acercarme primero a niños blancos recién nacidos. Siguiendo las directrices de la gran negra bruja apostada en la hacienda de la catedral Porta Coeli de los dominicos, los he santiguado y medicado contra los dolores de panza. Embadurno mis manos de mejunjes y coloco yerbas anestésicas en sus encías cuando les nacen los dientes. Los he puesto a mamarme los senos hasta que sale leche, para convertirme en su nodriza. Les hago cuentos, los desenredo con sus peines de plata, les abombacho las faldas de niñas de bien y los pantalones de señorito. Cocino para ellos, confecciono sus teses. Ordeño las ubres de sus vacas o cabras preferidas para darles de beber cuando gatean, o empiezan a caminar.

Voy ganando confianza. Todas las que hacen lo mismo que yo—y somos muchas—vamos ganando confianza. Entonces me inicio, ayudando a traer al mundo a los hijos de negras esclavas bozales. Son las negras más difíciles de domar, según los blancos. Yo soy en esencia una de ellas, pero me comporto como ladina. Hablo el español, visto de faldas y enaguas, incluso cuando trabajo de labranza en los campos, sé arrodillarme en las misas y ante las procesiones de vírgenes católicas inventadas. Nadie sabe que hablo lo que hablan los hausa, o los fulani, ni que me escondo detrás de las paredes a escuchar el acento de mis amos y sus visitas de milicia, para luego practicarlos en soledad.

Durante el veinteavo día de mi quinto encarcelamiento, se me extrae de la celda para adjudicarme los castigos físicos designados a mi condena. En el libro de la plantación aparecen anotadas todas mis infracciones: desobediencia, conducta desafiante, insolencia, vagancia excesiva, e incitación a revueltas y, en última instancia, las fugas. Ahora también esto, lo más grave. Una mestiza, a quien reconozco por haber estado en el último de los partos que oficié, amarra mis manos detrás de la espalda. Me empuja. Me escupe. El verdugo afirma que soy parte de una raza animal, sin alma ni corazón. Un sacerdote declama los rezos del rosario que con tanta abnegación nos han enseñado en la casa de nuestros señores. Me ordena en castellano que los repita con él. Al principio rehúso, hasta que inician los azotes.

Recuerdo que el chamán de aldea entonaba una cantata para invocar las protecciones contra el dolor. Mentalmente juego a que los padrenuestros y las avemarías hacen eso mismo. En un postrero intento de resistencia, logro desatarme las piernas y me arrastro maniatada. Me detienen algunos oficiales que me golpean más fuerte y que piden permiso para duplicar la flagelación. Pero un alto funcionario parece indicarles que no y no lo hacen. No me pegan más.

De vuelta al calabozo, durante el recorrido, reconozco a Petro, que camina a mi lado. Me extiende su mano y yo se la doy. Escucho que he sido sentenciada a morir en la horca. Entonces me desmayo.

8.

A petición mía, Petro describe los últimos tres atardeceres que ha logrado ver desde algún balcón de la ciudad amurallada. *L'orange, la vanille, roze*. Sobretodo rosado. Le cuento que en mi aldea, los niños que nacen como él, y con los ojos de su color, son adorados y se les obsequia, a ellos y a sus padres, hasta que acumulan una pequeña riqueza. De grandes, son cortejados por los guerreros más valerosos del recinto y luego cedidos en matrimonio a los merecedores. Las primeras y segundas esposas de los guerreros colaboran en la selección.

La tarde en que toca mi sentencia, alguien debe raparme la cabeza. Petro pide permiso al monasterio de frailes al que pertenece para que le permitan oficiar y así poder brindarme los santos óleos. Pero resulta que no soy bautizada y el asunto se desintegra. Al menos le permiten acompañarme en la procesión para subir hasta el patíbulo donde la cuerda me espera. Petro ve que permanezco impávida, me toma del rostro y repite el ritual confesionario. "Ave María Purísima". "Sin pecado concebida", contesto. "Dime tus pecados", mi niña.

Cierro los ojos y las lágrimas no caen. "¡No tengo ninguno!", exclamo. Él me abraza, improvisa un rito de cruces, trata de mantenerme de pie. Los asistentes observan: lugartenientes, capitanes de barco, hacendados y sus esposas, púberas y chiquitines con miras a heredar alguna hacienda, una docena de negras comadronas acusadas por primera o segunda vez y los oficiales que las escoltan censuradores con la esperanza de que por mi condena escarmienten. Una nodriza blanca, de bebé blanco, me rapa el cabello frente a todos. Los dueños que han perdido mercancías por mi culpa, aplauden.

"Ndizi, ¿qué les hiciste?; necesito que esta y las demás atrocidades se sepan". "Es mi secreto de confesión, padrecito", digo, "perdóneme". Y él insiste: "¿qué te tengo que perdonar?"

Un silencio.

Y una revelación. En decibeles bajos, en dialecto nuestro, mío y de Fray Petro, le digo: "Los ahogo en el balde de recolectar placentas, padrecito. Presiono sus negras gargantitas con mis dedos y los sofoco. O les asfixio con sus cordones umbilicales, incluso maniobrando antes que salgan del vientre. La madre no se da cuenta, o lo prefiere, o lo ha pedido... suplicando en lengua desconocida para el blanco. El acto, que puede ser muy sutil, pasa desapercibido por el velador de recién nacidos, que vigila procurando la sobrevivencia del futuro esclavo. Lo burlo. Lo burlamos. Si no puedo hacerlo durante el parto, más tarde les doy de comer frutos contaminados con sangre de mujeres con el tétano de las cadenas. O recojo diarreas expulsadas con pujos de disentería y las mezclo en las comidas y purés. A veces coloco el mejunje sobre el pezón de mis tetas y los lacto. O deposito casabe sin humedecer cerca de sus amígdalas y obstruyo las narices. No soy la única. Muchas me siguen. Hemos logrado un ejército".

Otro silencio.

Hago un recuento mental de palabras olvidadas. Replico sus sonidos. Articulo tocando el dorso de la lengua con la parte posterior del velo del paladar. Se forma una estrechez por la que pasa el aire aspirado. El aire no me llega. Siento mi úvula en medio de un resplandor. Soy toda una contracción vibratoria. Soy una faringe que se ahoga; luna, energía, coraje, eternidad.

Lo último que distingo son sus ojos rosados.

Even the smallest victory is never to be taken for granted. Each victory must be applauded.

—Audre Lorde

Saeta

1.

El amo camina con aire vacilante alrededor de las dos esclavas. Se deshace de las botas una por una y parece detener su andar en la observancia de las sombras de las paredes. No lo hace; no se detiene. Se desamarra la bombacha de los listones del cuello, y sigue dando vueltas alrededor de la habitación iluminada tan solo por las velas. Luego, más decidido, termina por tocarle los abundantes senos a Tshanwe y ella baja el rostro. La llama Teresa, pero ella no sabe por qué.

El cabello prieto, ensortijado, no le cae sobre la cara a Tshanwe, y la blusa que el amo levanta no está hecha de hilos importados. Con todo, él parece disfrutar la diferencia de carnes firmes y joviales que ya no porta su mujer, pero que sí encuentra al ras de esta piel oscura. La condesa ha dado a luz siete de sus vástagos y se dedica últimamente al mundillo. Esta actividad que se gesta dentro de las alcobas no le ha hecho bien a su constitución por la falta de ejercicio. Su permanencia en la residencia colonial la tiene pálida y con los músculos temblones. Cuando mueve las extremidades para cerrar las cortinas de la estancia principal, la carne fofa del antebrazo se le derrama trepidante del mismo modo en que lo hacen la superficie de los dulces que cocina la esclava Jwaabi al fogón. Los dulces son tembluscos y se remenean, tanto en los calderos como en las vasijas. La esclava los prepara siguiendo las órdenes del propio conde, que a su vez, exige las golosinas criollas confeccionadas bajo la rigurosidad de un recetario indígena que ha traído uno de sus amigos desde la capital.

El amo desprende la falda manchada de barro de Tshanwe y, con una mano, le abre las piernas. La vuelve a llamar Teresa. Palpa su pubis, y lo estudia con ávidos ojos. Varios de sus dedos se hacen enredos con él. Empuja a la negra hasta el lecho, no sin antes retirar el mosquitero. Entonces entra y sale de ella; entra y sale.

La otra esclava, Jwaabi, se ha quedado de pie, en mitad del aposento, con las manos entrelazadas a la espalda. Espera sin pudor su turno.

2.

La mañana en que el perro del señorito Gregorio murió, Tshanwe ayudaba a Jwaabi a rayar las verduras. No comprendió del todo lo que ocurría. Tshanwe había sido la última adquisición del conde don Georgino Pizarro en el mercado de esclavos capitalino, y por lo mismo no hablaba nada de la lengua de los amos.

Tampoco reconocía los códices indígenas de aquellos que llamaban taínos y cuya lengua parecía ser tan necesaria para la cocción de alimentos. Había sido separada de sus consanguíneos en su tierra natal y apenas había sobrevivido el viaje en nao. Mucho menos entendía el lenguaje nativo de Jwaabi, ni el de los demás sirvientes que se hacían cargo del mantenimiento de la hacienda Pizarro puesto que casi todos venían de etnias diferentes dispersadas en el gran continente.

Tshanwe reconocía pocas palabras, incluso cuando éstas se decían con lentitud; "ven", "comida", "castigo". Por otro lado, sí reconocía el llamado de la negra Jwaabi. En el momento en que la ama gritaba "Juana", Tshanwe veía como Jwaabi corría a su lado para atender a alguno de los críos o para ayudarla con la palangana. La condesa tenía fobia por los excrementos, y la sola idea de tocarlos al parecer le revolvía las tripas. Era por ello que ni siquiera ella misma limpiaba su trasero. Vociferaba "¡Juana!", luego de culminar su asunto, y la esclava salía de prisa a asearla y a retirar las heces depositadas en el recipiente. Tshanwe suponía que "Juana" y Jwaabi eran la misma cosa.

Esa mañana, mientras todavía hacían preparativos en la cocina, Tshanwe escuchó que el señorito Gregorio hablaba alto desde la sala. Hablaba y soltaba sollozos. Insistía en mencionar la frase "Está muerto; nadie sabe cómo". Lloraba desde el fondo del pecho, con un llanto que llamó la atención a la recién llegada y a sus ojos curiosos, con un llanto que nunca le había escuchado a ninguno de los jovencitos de su aldea, a excepción del día de las detonaciones. Tshanwe escudriñó al señorito por detrás de la cortina, entre ocultándose y dejándose ver un poco. Estudió al perro que no respiraba sobre las maderas del piso. Miró al amo Georgino y supuso que regañaba al muchachito. Le habló con voz fuerte, y volvió a mencionar "muerto". El señorito repitió "no sé". Tshanwe se retiró a la cocina, y antes de proseguir cortando las verduras por instrucciones gestuales de la otra negra, le hizo a una mueca.

—¿Muerto?

Jwaabi asintió con la cabeza, todavía cercenando una posta. Tshanwe le

tomó la cara e hizo una seña de pregunta, asegurándose esta vez de que la miraba.

—¿Muerto?

Jwaabi habló en su dialecto. Se alzó de hombros. En vista de que el rostro dubitativo continuaba,

abrió las palmas de las manos y las meneó.

—Nadie sabe cómo.

3.

Tshanwe fue elegida una tarde para cargar todas las ballestas—la del amo y la de cada invitado—hasta el lugar desde donde los hombres practicaban sus cualidades gallardas. Era un llano empinado que se perdía detrás de la hacienda, un poco más allá del monte de cañas. Al principio el cargamento se le hizo insoportable, pero luego se acostumbró al peso y pudo llegar. Después de comenzados los lanzamientos de flecha hacia la variada arboleda en derredor, Tshanwe se mantuvo de pie divisando el silencio del cielo. Trajo a la memoria la mañana de la muerte del perro.

Ese día había esperado a que dos de los esclavos mudaran al animal sin vida a las caballerizas. Lo habían colocado en una mesa en espera de poder hacer un hoyo en la tierra para enterrarlo. Los negros se movieron hacia el lugar en donde se enterraban, por órdenes de los condes, a los animales muertos y a los esclavos fallecidos. Mientras cavaban, Tshanwe se había acercado al animal y lo había palpado. Descubrió sangre en uno de los costados y espulgando más su pelaje, dio con un agujero en su piel. El agujero no era tan profundo, lo palpó hasta el fondo con su dedo índice. Descubrió un pedazo de algo incrustado. Decidida a saciar su sed de indagaciones, maniobró con el cadáver y sus uñas, hasta lograr extirpar el pedazo. Era el cabezal de una saeta.

Tshanwe la guardó como amuleto.

Se preguntaba si aquello que se pronunciaba "nadiesabecómo" querría decir precisamente eso. Por lo que había entendido, "no sé", "nadie sabe" o "nosécómo" significaban algo así como desconocimiento. Lo había deducido por el levantamiento de hombros de los demás

4.

La madrugada del aniversario de boda de los condes, el amo salió muy temprano, despuntando el alba, a practicar con el arco. Pero antes, efectuaría otra acción. Había levantado del cuarto de las esclavas a Tshanwe y a la cocinera. Se las había llevado hasta el cobertizo. En esa ocasión, mientras murmuraba la palabra "Juana", había entrado en Jwaabi primero, dejando a la otra que observara. Luego se había servido de Tshanwe, llamándola Teresa. Finalizado el acto, tomó a Tshanwe del brazo y la arrastró hasta el cuarto reservado para las armas. Le colocó el bolso de flechas a un lado y una de sus dos ballestas en el otro.

Entonces caminó al frente de ella, dirigiéndola hasta el talud.

Quizás lo traicionó la hora—era demasiado temprano—, pero el conde se cansó pronto y regresó a la hacienda. Quizás lo traicionó la bebida aquella que se tragaba en abundancia, directo de la vejiga de cuero que cargaba casi siempre con él.

Dejó a Tshanwe sola, rodeada de las mariposas y los grillos, en aquel verdor colmado de azules por la poca luminosidad de la mañana. Tshanwe se dejó caer a tierra, extenuada. Dormitó sobre el rocío de la hierba apenas unos instantes. Sin embargo, casi de inmediato, se irguió. Antes de decidir colocarse los pesados bultos de vuelta sobre los hombros para regresar, tomó el arco y lo cargó. Musitó "nadie sabe cómo" previo a lanzar la flecha hacia la lejanía de los árboles.

5.

La festividad de los condes terminó como el rosario de la aurora cuando Trino, el señorito mayor, ensayó un fallido intento de lucha gladiadora con su padre, un poco antes de la puesta de sol. Comenzaron tirando puños al aire, en medio de un juego de licores y carcajadas. Pasaron luego a agarrarse las cabezas entre los brazos y el costado rival, dando seguidos traspiés, apretándose casi hasta la asfixia. De repente atisbó un gran empujón de uno de ellos y el grupo de nudillos del más joven impactó la mejilla del más viejo.

Algo de alboroto se escuchó hasta en las afueras. Don Georgino, acostumbrado a la hidalguía que dosificaba el aguante, se deshizo en un altisonante grito al que se le unieron varios gemidos como los de una mula.

Mientras la condesa intervenía, con un paño que trajo Tshanwe para detener el profuso sangrado, los compañeros de caza del conde lo socorrieron evitando que éste, mareado, cayera al suelo. Tshanwe se quedó perpleja observando el brillo de la sangre, lo mojado de su consistencia, el color y la espesura de esta sangre tan parecida a otras, la semejanza del fluido que brotaba del hombre blanco casi del mismo modo con que lo hacía la de los hombres y las mujeres de su Namaqua.

6.

Esa noche, en el rincón forrado de tierra que hacía las veces de cama, jugó con la idea de regresar alguna vez a los suyos, de verlos envejecer entre los sabios y sus magias, de tocarles el rostro tatuado con los colores de las plantas al otro lado del desierto. Trajo a la memoria ese mismo desierto, el de Namib y a sus dunas de arena que tantas veces sirvieron de escondite a ella y a sus parientes con los juegos de aldea. Recordó los sonidos de chasquido tan peculiares del lenguaje de su localidad, y cómo Namaqua celebraba la llegada de recién nacidos con golosinas confeccionadas del fruto de las palmeras. Se dio vuelta en el lecho y alcanzó la punta de su nuevo amuleto. Lo acarició con la yema de uno de sus dedos. Emitió un silbido, que se fundió entre la noche y el ruido de las ranas. Si alguien le contestara el silbido, si tan solo alguien lo hiciera. . .

La sensación le trajo remembranzas de cuando escuchaba la señal de las mujeres de Namaqua anunciando algún evento de guerra. Se pintaban debajo de los ojos y sobre la nariz con una pasta hecha de especias en tonos que conmemoraban el amanecer. Colocaban en un amarre a sus espaldas la lanza y las otras armas de combate. Eran llamadas por los demás pueblos las cazadoras amarillas, famosas por usar flechas envenenadas, a lo largo y a lo ancho de la meseta del interior. Mujeres que desconocían el temor. O al menos no lo habían conocido hasta que se volvieron, ellas y sus familias, presas de criaturas más claras de piel que llegaban en barcazas y que las encadenaban. Las ataban con sortilegios. El encantamiento consistía en hacer detonar la carne para lograr las rendiciones. El sueño finalmente la venció.

7.

La habían acorralado. La esquina la cobijó por un rato, por muy poco tiempo la verdad, justo hasta que los señoritos se le acercaron amenazadores disminuyendo el cerco. La habían asaltado por sorpresa. Llegaba del campo de tiro de acompañar al conde y todavía tenía en sus hombros las marcas que las tiras de los bultos le habían dibujado por cargarlos. Esa tarde, como tantas otras en las que planeaba fugarse un rato de vuelta a la planicie inclinada, los dos acorraladores se le habían puesto de frente. Fueron empujándola en contra de su voluntad, movidos por la intimidación que aguantaba uno en la mano derecha y el otro en la izquierda. El grande, Trino, quien apenas le superaba en estatura, utilizaba un instrumento muy parecido al amuleto de Tshanwe, partido a la mitad y puntiagudo. A modo de florete lo acercaba y lo retiraba con un fortuito movimiento de muñeca. Gregorio portaba entre sus dedos una de las agujas de mundillo de la condesa y la meneaba hasta que ésta se espetaba en algún muslo, el brazo, la pantorrilla de la piel negra.

Tshanwe abrió y cerró los ojos. Intentó convocar espíritus protectores, sin éxito. Esquivó nuevamente la amenaza de Trino justo en el momento en que Gregorio volvía a hacerla sangrar por la parte baja de la axila. Escuchó las voces de los muchachos decirle "eres como un perro", "la sangre de los negros no es igual", pero desconocía los significados.

Entonces se movió hacia el frente, intentando correr aunque estuviese lastimada. En ese preciso instante, Trino no falló. Apenas lo esquivó, pero aún así la flecha partida le rayó la cara. Gregorio aprovechó para estirar la aguja, y se la espetó en la palma de la mano abierta. Tan pronto le brotó más líquido morado, ambos exclamaron: "¡sangra de verdad!".

No se detienen. Continúan espetando los filos. Estos entran y salen sin compasión. Los senos, el cuello, el abdomen de la esclava se marcan de rayas como tatuajes. Los tatuajes hacen correr el líquido cálido, le hacen caer de rodillas debilitada.

Maniobra por una milésima de aliento y le arrebata, aun estando encorvada, el afilado instrumento de manos de Trino. Descarta,—como posible repercusión de su defensa—las ideas del calabozo, el cadalso, la viga del cepo en donde se aprisionan manos y pies, y la soga estirándole el cuello y las extremidades por uno de los caballos del amo. Aunque tales imágenes le nublan, por un momento, la razón, las desecha de inmediato. En aquel, su primer acto de defensa, intentando persuadirlos para que la dejen en paz, Tshanwe esgrime el puntiagudo objeto hacia el señorito de mayor estatura, de modo que la parte metálica de la saeta termina incrustándose en el dedo corazón de él. Trino comienza a dar alaridos, acaparando la atención de su hermano menor. Fue cuestión de tiempo; la aparición de la figura del conde en presencia del trío.

Una lluvia de puños y patadas a su rostro fueron el inicio de la paliza que recibiría de parte del amo. Lo ve detenerse y vociferar a los chicos. Recibe más golpes en el torso. "Valen caro los esclavos"; "es mi propiedad". Golpes a la espalda. "¡Muchachos insensatos!", "vas a ver quién manda, negra asquerosa". Tshanwe no entiende y cae impotente al suelo. Nota entre sollozos cómo el amo golpea también a los señoritos. Ve cómo el rostro del conde se cuaja al notar la herida del vástago, su preocupación, su ira. Al principio logra una posición fetal sobre el piso que la protege de algunas fracturas. No así de las dislocaciones de hombros y caderas que llegan después. La vejiga de cuero vacía de licores rueda por el suelo. A la escaramuza de golpes se le unen la de los señoritos y los de algunos acompañantes de ballesta de don Georgino. Tshanwe pierde la noción.

8.

Ágil como gacela, libre sobre la estepa del imponente paisaje rocoso de su tierra. Así corre, así escapa. Se embadurna de pinturas bélicas que anuncian tempestad de dardos y pértigas. Salta por encima de la extensión de piedra arenisca que oscila más allá de las huellas de dinosaurio grabadas en su superficie.

Desfila en un letargo por el bosque selvático, hábitat del petrificado enemigo. Chasquidos de lengua y una orden de ejecución en masa. Silbidos que contestan silbidos. Tshanwe se prohíbe expirar; se prohíbe fenecer. La voluntad de sus ancestros y su temple la dirigen de vuelta por el túnel. No fallezcas, odalisca. No perezcas, gladiadora. El tiempo de las edades pasadas te reclama. El agua transportando pinos a esa tierra árida y enterrándolos en el lodo durante el transcurso de los siglos, exige tu existencia. Millares de cebras, antílopes y núes, miríadas de elefantes, leones y jirafas marcan el carnaval de las heridas, lamiendo la carne descompuesta luego de la batalla.

Los ríos se han convertido en arena. Las corrientes de agua no son más que hoyos fangosos infectados. Miles de cabezas de ganado vacuno, cabras, ovejas y camellos se han rendido y caído para morir sobre la tierra reseca y quebrada que ya no acoge a los pechos amamantando. Ahora esa tierra tiene sobreabundancia de escasez; sus hijas le han sido arrebatadas.

9.

Otros dos esclavos fortachones que tampoco se entienden entre sí, pero que ya aprenden poco a poco la lengua de los amos, cargan de los brazos y las piernas a Tshanwe. Siguen las instrucciones del conde de enterrarla en el lugar de los perros y los negros. Como comienza a llover, la colocan sobre una plataforma de madera en donde nadie le rinde tributos ni actos de duelo. Allí la dejan a solas por varias horas, y se van a hacer otros quehaceres, esperando que con el paso de la tarde el aguacero mengüe y así puedan cavar su hoyo para depositarla, antes que la carne se descomponga y comience a apestar.

Las gotas le reaniman los párpados y un chamán invisible la hace despertar. Namaqua y sus mujeres guerreras la amparan. Desaparece el cuerpo. también desaparece una de las ballestas del amo. Tres días más tarde, nadie se explica el encantamiento. Nadie comprende el embrujo. El amo y sus hombres arrojan primero sus propias flechas hacia la floresta, como tienen por costumbre. Otra mañana de ejercicios de flechas. Algún acto de hechicería hace regresar a una de ellas, como un bumerán. La saeta disparada a través de la arboleda al final del llano emite un silbido. Los espíritus—es la única explicación—lo contestan. Logra incrustarse en la frente de don Georgino. Nadie sabe cómo.

Los amamantados

1.

Para Petra es difícil aceptar las actuales acciones del señorito. Desde que cumpliera lo que se considera la mayoría de edad para un joven hacendado, sus intereses han ido cambiando. Mientras fue un bebé pálido, regordete y feliz, que sonreía nada más acercarle Petra sus pechos pletóricos de alimento, nunca hubo problema. Tampoco ha sido problemático para la esclava canalizar la ansiedad que le ocasiona al señorito ir a la escuela en San Juan. El primer día que ingresa al aula de los famosos maestros apellidados Cordero, le comienza una erupción en la piel.

En la sala de clases a la que han asignado al pequeño Jonás, hay otros niños del latifundio, muchachos y muchachas de buenas familias blancas, propietarios a su vez de esclavos, peones y capataces. La mayoría son conocidos del señorito, han jugado juntos, entrenan esgrima y montura a caballo, asisten a fiestas y bailes, en las afueras y en las propiedades cercanas de la zona. Tanto el Maestro Rafael, como su hermana Celestina, imparten clases a otros niños negros, algunos de origen bozal; otros son mulatos, mestizos y hasta cuarterones nacidos en la isla, pero no mezclan los grupos de púberes morenos con los mozos blancos, por lo que se descarta enseguida que el padecimiento es motivado al estar en contacto directo con criaturas bestializadas como aquellas. Así pues, el boticario diagnostica una condición de desapego, provocada por el cambio de ambiente.

La dueña de la Hacienda Cartagena, ama y señora a su vez de Petra, ordena de inmediato que la negra ladina acompañe al señorito a sus clases diarias, se estampe a las puertas del patio interior de la residencia Cordero, y ofrezca la teta al chiquillo cada vez que este lo requiera. Petra obedece e incluso sale beneficiada con el arreglo, ya que en las horas de espera, no realiza mayores trabajos que no sean el tejido de los ropajes de lana de su amamantado, Jonás Cartagena. Además, se le debe tener a disposición alimentos en buen estado y abundantes candungos de agua, para que la leche que ella prodiga al querubín, sea cuantiosa y de la mejor calidad de nutrientes. La comezón provocada por el sarpullido del jovencito desaparece al cabo de unos días.

2.

Petra ha nacido en San Juan Bautista y es descendiente mandinga por vía de su abuela materna, contado por ella misma en noches de nanas y corroborado cuando el propio señorito cuestiona el origen de los esclavos que le pertenecen, al Maestro Cordero. Con atípica obsesión, y mientras ha ido creciendo en estatura y años, Jonás insiste en discutir varias veces el tema de su procedencia. Es así como se familiariza con una cartografía encontrada en el despacho de su fallecido padre, en la que se demarcan los territorios entre Cabo Banco y Cabo Las Palmas, Senegal, Cabo Verde y Sierra Leona en el continente africano. Y es así como Celestina Cordero con paciencia le va explicando la ruta de tránsito para saciar la curiosidad púber. Recuerda el muchacho, el día que en secreto hace una pregunta al pequeño grupo de jovencitos blancos que como él se educan. Inquiere sobre el servicio de las negras esclavas; cuestiona por qué se les estima a algunas de ellas, si debieran ser bestias de carga, si debieran ser inferiores. Interpela incluso sobre la abolición, un tema que ha escuchado por lo bajo a algunos hombres cuando se dirigen a las tabernas. «Abolicionista», palabra comprometedora aquella. Crecer y luchar por el bien de todas y de todos. Liberar a seres no liberados. Forjar un mejor mundo.

Plantea cuestionamientos porque no entiende. Pero otro de los chicos, en voz baja, le contesta: «Dice mi padre que las negras están aquí solo para montarlas. Se disfrutan mejor que las blancas». Jonás Cartagena reacciona sorprendido, y ya no es el mismo.

3.

Así pues, las fijaciones del señorito ahora no se centran necesariamente en mamar las ubres a Petra para procurar alimentación. De un tiempo a esta parte, el muchacho alto y fornido de catorce años, que ya va tomando las riendas de la hacienda heredada, asedia en las noches el cuarto de las esclavas y en ocasiones, incluso, se detiene en silencio muy cerca del catre de hojarasca de Petra.

Ella lo ha visto y se hace la dormida y continúa respirando como si roncara, para dar la impresión de que desconoce aquellas intenciones. Durante el día, se da cuenta también que el señorito la sigue a escondidas, que se le acerca para olerla mientras ella lacta a otros bebés españoles y criollos, que le toca las piernas por cualquier excusa, que la dibuja en pedazos de papel que luego esconde para restregárselos por todo el cuerpo cuando yace solo.

La semana pasada Jonás se colocó en un lugar estratégico entre el cuarto de lavado y unos matorrales. Petra percibió su presencia cuando ya era demasiado tarde y el señorito frotaba hacia atrás y hacia adelante el pedazo de carne y piel con el que los hombres blancos violan a las de su especie.

4.

Pasados unos cuantos días, Petra es asignada a ejercer de nodriza a los mellizos recién nacidos de la hermana de su ama y señora, madre del propio Jonás. La ama desea que sus sobrinos crezcan y se desarrollen con tan buena disposición y tan buen talante corporal, como lo habían logrado con el adolescente hacendado.

La tarde del bautismo de los gemelos, los entregan a Petra para que los alimente al mismo tiempo, en su regazo.

Después de amamantar a los chiquillos, Petra atestigua cómo se los llevan en medio de un séquito celebratorio dirigido a la catedral. Todos los integrantes de la familia Cartagena y varios de los oficiales de la hacienda se dirigen hacia los actos sacramentales que, según tenía entendido, realizaría el propio señor obispo. Todos regresan tarde, rompiendo el alba, ya que luego del bautizo habría comilona. Todos menos Jonás, que vuelve al par de horas, solo.

Petra teje, a luz de vela, dos pares de botines para los mellizos en una de las alcobas. Le molestan los senos; más bien le duelen, ya que al dar de amamantar a dos, sus pezones reciben la doble estimulación típica de estos casos y se precipitan a expulsar el calostro. Le chorrea leche por todo el vientre.

El señorito llega. Abre y cierra todas las puertas. Busca en todas las habitaciones. Se le queda mirando al hallarla. Acerca sus pasos hasta el sillón y de un movimiento de manos, con sus dedos, desamarra los cordones de la blusa de algodón confeccionada especialmente para las negras amamantadoras. Petra cierra los ojos, vencida. Incrédula ante el nuevo vejamen que ahora la convierte en algo diferente para aquel niño.

Jonás palpa las tetas de alabastro, de color jaspe oscuro. Pechos mandingas, de sabor meloso, presos de un caudillaje senegalés se yerguen frente a él. Pieles descendientes de algún imperio guerrero. Ha leído sobre los ancestros de Petra en el Documento de Cartas de las Indias y Nuevas Colonias de 1793. Se lo ha memorizado. Desea en cualquier ocasión regalarle aquel detalle de conocimiento a Petra. Quiere recitarlo. Cantarlo si hubiera la oportunidad y fuera posible. Decírselo a ella y a su cintura. A sus muslos. A los senos negrísimos. Jonás se arrodilla, y ante la cascada cremosa pega sus labios. Se los echa a la boca. Succiona fuerte y comienza a mamar, mientras cubiertas las mejillas de lágrimas, le abre las piernas.

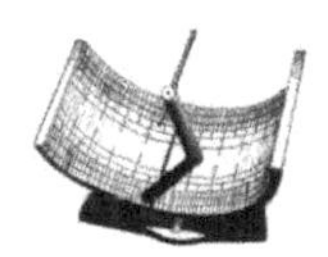

Yo, Makandal

Poemas

Seré Makandal
en los ungüentos de plantas
que guerrearán las venas
del imperialista yanki anglo
que encadena a mi pueblo mulato
a la esclavitud de la droga y el viernes negro
de empresas extranjeras

Seré Makandal Albizu
en la mañana en que las campanas
dejarán su té de veneno pardo
en las gargantas de los amos
en el congreso o Casa Blanca
donde todavía se trafican seres humanos

—Raúl Guadalupe

Génesis de un poemario

LA AVENTURA de escribir este libro comenzó cuando inicié estudios doctorales en 2016 animada por gente a la que amo y admiro: Miguel Rodríguez López, Luis López Nieves, Sandra Guzmán, Manuel Figueroa, Zulma Oliveras Vega y Waleska Semidey. Mi hermano del alma e hijo adoptivo que la vida me ha regalado, el escritor David Caleb Acevedo, me acababa de recomendar que escribiera un diario a modo de balancear mis emociones debido a algunas complicaciones melancólicas y románticas que enfrentaba mi vida. Fue así como me di a la tarea de retomar la escritura reflexiva diaria para entender y entenderme. Con el paso del tiempo, y añadida la singularidad de que el Dr. Raúl Guada-lupe, mi profesor de los cursos HILI 1012 Historia y literatura afrodescendiente y HILI 1009 Problemas de la historia y la literatura puertorriqueñas en el siglo XX nos retara a escribir una reflexión dialógica semanal para su clase, este libro poco a poco y sin querer fue tomando forma. Todos esos escritos nacieron o fueron convertidos en reacciones poéticas que incluía yo a los trabajos que asignaba el Dr. Guadalupe. También fui añadiendo algunas contestaciones creativas provocadas por el curso del Dr. Josué Santiago, LITE 1611 Literatura Antillana I: De los mitos taínos hasta el Modernismo. A su vez, la lectura de uno de los mejores libros que a mi entender se ha escrito sobre el tema, El evangelio de Makandal y los hacedores de lluvia del propio Raúl Guadalupe, publicado en 2015 por Editorial Tiempo Nuevo, me dio el resto de la inspiración que necesitaba junto a los sucesos políticos y de interés general que giraron en torno a mi vida durante esta época tan incierta en que mi corazón se dividía tanto por un cisma romántico, como por un desarraigo social. El poema de Raúl Guadalupe que sirve de epígrafe para este libro, y que da inicio al mismo, fue una de las lecciones más oportunas que estaba yo recibiendo de la vida. Yo acababa de entregar una monografía a Guadalupe sobre *El reino de este mundo* de Alejo Carpentier en medio de un vórtice de conflictos originados por el racismo descarado y rampante que arropa a Puerto Rico, y la tendencia de *blackface* que parecía querer regresar a los medios de comunicación como un bumerán ancestral y opresor. Así que junto a la monografía, le entregué al profesor un poema desahogo titulado El reino de esta mofa que luego de algunas transformaciones vino a convertirse en el poema *Yo, Makandal*. Cuando Raúl Guadalupe me devolvió el trabajo corregido, en la retro-alimentación que brinda al pie de las páginas, y en puño y letra, había escrito esa contestación/ poema. Repito, para mí fue una gran lección. Era como si el profesor me estuviese diciendo: "Sigue, poeta. Siente. Vive. Escribe, que siempre prevalece la poesía".

Bendito el día en que sea una mujer la que caiga defendiendo la libertad de su patria. Ese día habrá una revolución en cada hogar portorriqueño y se reconocerá en pleno la grandeza de nuestra justa causa.

—Julia de Burgos

El Reino

Yo, Makandal

Seré Makandal
guerrera transmutada en el género que sea necesario
para destronar este racismo
que tanto nos pone en falta
en carencias
en desdichas
que nos atormenta y humilla
destronaré a los blancos que se pintan el rostro
aquellos que aún hoy se burlan de mi etnia
de mi raza
mi color
mis bembas grandes palesianas
mi piel oscura mozambiquea y juliaburguesina
mis caderas cual Quimbamba
cual Tembandumba macheteando de cuajo el blackface

Seré Makandal
guerrera transmutada
carnavalesca
mosquito sobre la cabeza del racista rey, presidente
  o gobernante
picadura mortal para que ya no se pinte
para que ya no se burle
para que entienda el dolor causado
primero por sus cadenas
luego por su risa estéril de mi existencia
desestabilizadora

Seré Makandal
y mi dominio será esta patria de discrimen
  y desigualdad
que convertiré en antirracista, en abolicionista
porque se nos va la vida
a mí, a mis hermanos de lucha, a nuestros hijos
  y nietos por venir
al reino de este mundo

Tembandumba de la Yolanda

Tembandumba usurpa mis bembes
me abre una antilla en el pecho
una plantación de esclavos en cada pezón
latigazos en cada palpitación

un barco negrero de madres oscuras
que se ahogan ellas mismas
para así evitar al mayoral y al amo
para así evitar la sodomía
la destrucción de matrices
los dolores de parto a jovencitas de diez

un Caribe que abanica mis labios grandes
una Tembandumba que atraca mi afro
rescata mi culo
estas caderas asesinas que culipandean sueños
estas nalgas voluntariosas
que me hacen ser existir
esa Tembandumba que ha consolado mi tristeza acosada
que se ha regodeado en la crueldad de los burlones
en la mofa de quienes no defienden
no reivindican
no se solidarizan

castigo a los de tez blanca que oprimen
y a los de tez oscura que sudan complicidad
a quienes imitan el hablar de una negra desconocida
sonoridad de época arcaica
objeto de risa
ruidos de lengua que no me identifican
esa Tembandumba no quiere ser negroide
no cree en la negra maldad de canciones preciosas

soy negra,
soy estas bembas hermosamente ordinarias
soy negra,
soy este afro abultado sin alisar
soy explayá, ensanchada, esparcida, denunciadora
soy rizos encaracolados
alentados por surcos de trenzas
enmarañados con el ruido de tambores hechos
    mapas de escape
trenzas liberadoras

soy Tun Tún afroantillana
de pasa y grifería
con rumba, macumba, candombe, bámbula
entre unas filas afroboricuas
soy calabó
deidad bambú

mano azabache
prieta cachonda que al Congo clama
soy negra Tembandumba, maestro Palés
soy grifa y pura negra, maestra Julia
soy Guillén, Carpentier, Calibán, Makandal
soy de la Encendida Calle Antillana.

Yo, Calibán

Calibán tempestiva soy
una nueva criatura
Calibán de senos y vagina
caníbal de tus labios
que trago esa boca
en medio de este vaivén
vomito en lágrimas el deseo de emancipación
prospero en mi lucha
lucho contra Próspero
en la voluntad de ser libre
de liberar a mis ancestros ahogados estatuas de sal
debajo del mar
hombres y mujeres mandíbulas
quienes abrieron sus dientes para engullir las vísceras
del esclavizador
y tú fuiste amo
yo soy tu ama hoy
domino tu piel blanca que te obsesiona domino esa
dermis con mi sexo
soy Mayoral
soy látigo, mejunje, carimbo
y qué soy
babalao soy
sacerdotisa en una isla sin naufragios sin náufragos

lograré la venganza
al alcanzar el orgasmo
observando mi triunfo
gozándome tu destrucción

prosperar en medio de estos vientos engullir esta
tempestad para liberar a los míos

soy Calibán
Calibana
Canibalia
caribeña
tu corazón yace crudo entre mis colmillos
ya baja en carne viva por mi garganta

Yelidá

ese ardor en la boca quisqueyana
es la sal esparcida
la herida en carne viva
y una lágrima fugaz
ante el contoneo de la espalda

otro latigazo
y juraré vengarme
ponerme fuerte
aprender tu lengua
embaucarte con mi vudú
una magia en petición orisha
un hechizo en cacofonía ashanti

aquella mujer Isla
varona entregada al cuerpo oscuro
desafiante
amestizada
boca de blanca entre bembas negras
pestañas que sueñan en Togo y Benín en Sierra Leona,
    Brasil
Colombia, Cuba

un poema amulatado
un verso mulato
una Antilla mestiza
eres mi Ayití
eres la Española
eres la que se rebela

dos mitologías de sangre
Damballá
Queddó
Badagris
Legbá y Ogún
bésame el voudú delicioso
mientras corren por nuestro jardín caribeño
   los liliputienses infantiles de la nieve
los hiperbóreos duendes del trinco y del reno
la muchacha negra
la cabeza rubia
la playa noruega
afroantillana un día sí y un día no
blanca los otros

un antes
otro antes
un después

un paréntesis
otro después
un final

alma de araña para el macho cómplice Yelidá del espasmo
Yelidá del camino
Yelidá de su vientre
asesina del viento perdido entre los dientes
vegetal y ardiente
en húmeda humedad

Credo

Creo en Alejo Carpentier todopoderoso
creador del reino de este mundo
de todo lo visible y lo invisible
creo en su cosmos
en el universo paralelo
en la reencarnación de los karmas, los chacras y
el namasté
en su péndulo de Foucault
y en el ingenio de la lucha
en la protesta
en la denuncia
el no decaer
en los gritos que no se extinguen
hasta encontrar justicia
en la crucifixión de los traidores
que roban al vulgo
al pueblo oprimido por el imperio
a las mujeres asesinadas por el machismo

creo en su único Hijo Makandal
redentor y mesías yerbero
héroe de la magia y el vudú
creo en el paraíso de su manigua
en su palenque

en su quilombo
y que desde aquella tonga ha de venir a juzgar a vivos
y muertos
esclavizados y esclavistas
amos y abolicionistas
mayorales y latigadores
sodomizadores de infantes
nodrizas, caudillas y malinches
Makandal eres. . . dios de dios, luz de luz, dios verdadero
de dios verdadero, engendrado y mutilado
sin el brazo de la misma naturaleza del Padre, por quien
todo fue hecho
makandal serás, makandal seré; quien por nosotros los
hombres y por nuestra liberación bajó del cielo
y está sentado a la derecha del Padre; y de nuevo vendrá
con gloria para juzgar a vendepatrias y no macheteros
y su reino no tendrá fin

Creo en la tempestad
en Shakespeare y sus hijos de palabras
concebidos en al ardor de un Caribe ventoso
y huracanado
diosa caníbal
diseñadora de los gritos en mi garganta
del abuso a los cuerpos negros
de la mofa a los blancos que se pintan la piel

creo en Próspero, Montaigne y Ariel
trinidades usurpadoras de ducados
hijos de reyes que hacen el amor a Miranda
en las promesas de Nápoles
en las tetillas agujeradas de los homofóbicos
y el ornamento cruel que distingue la cabeza
de los racistas
nacidos en los campos de Puerto Rico
hacendados herederos con cosechas de naranjas
cabellos de pelo blanco en Castañer
pieles blancas marchitadas ante la abundancia
de cafetales
pieles poderosas
abusivas

Creo en Sycorax bruja madre
anhelante del hijo y sedienta de padre
creadora del Cielo y de la tierra
quien ha de aplastar a Trínculo
en los espacios de mis sueños de justicia
por obra y gracia del espíritu santo del dios africano
Orula

creo en la santa virgen de regla
y sus coágulos
creo en sus pujos de divinidad roja

que han de ahogar a los opresores en el mar de
sangre vaginal
creo en el beso a mi glande que es mi clítoris
y que mis súbditos deberán acariciar mis testículos
ovarios
para así callar la boca a los intolerantes

creo en los contaminados de Peñuelas
y en Tito Kayak
y en los presos políticos sin cárcel
que van todos los días a trabajar a cambio
de un salario mínimo
creo en los estudiantes
que padecen bajo el poder de Poncio Pilato Roselló
y en el duelo por el pueblo de esta isla
que ha sido masacrado, muerto y sepultado según
las escrituras
que descendió a los infiernos de una junta de
control fiscal
y que al tercer día resucitarán con sus machetes
Yo subiré a las nubes
y besaré a mis amantes
en poliamorosa conjunción
y me sentaré abierta de piernas
con mi vagina al viento
a la derecha del dios padre nadapoderoso

y derramaré un solo bautismo
desde mi hueco
sobre los rostros que así lo deseen
para el perdón de los pecados
y este reino tampoco tendrá fin
Creo en Nicolás Guillen, en Llorens Torres, en Palés
Matos y Corretjer
en el Espíritu Santo que es Julia de Burgos
en la santa Iglesia del país de cuatro pisos
cuyas columnas son Lolita Lebrón, Albizu Campos, Rafael
Cancel Miranda y Oscar López Rivera

creo en la comunión de los santos
en Hostos, Betances y Rodríguez de Tió
en el perdón de los pecados que implica regalar mis
playas a la privatización
a los intereses de los ricos
a los bancos, los hoteles y la milicia imperial
creo en la resurrección de la carne
la conversión de este zaguán en la República
de Puerto Rico
y la vida del mundo futuro
Amén.

Diosa te salve, Yemayá

Diosa te salve, Yemayá
llena eres de ashé
la babalawo sea contigo
bendita tus hijas que toman la justicia en sus manos
y bendito es el fruto de tu océano-río Oshún

Santa Yemayá
madre de diosas
consentidora de todos los amores
de todas las lenguas y enjambres de labios
de toda hembra que ama a otra mujer

Ave Purísima Yemayá
santificada por criar a nuestras hijas e hijos
y enseñarles a devolver el golpe del marido borracho
maltratador
abusador
llena eres de balas
y cuchillas
prestas para el ajusticiamiento

rueguen por nosotras los orishas
Obatalá
Orula madre y padre

los dioses del santo hermafroditismo Eleguá y los ángeles
transexuales
ahora y en la hora
de la libertad
de la desobediencia civil
de los defensores
de nuestra entrega por la patria
y nuestra bandera borincana
Amén

El día que murió Fidel

El día que murió Fidel
mi país se alimentaba de cenizas tóxicas
Las olas del mar en Peñuelas
se mecían rojas y espumosas
vaticinando el cáncer pulmonar
a la espera de la asfixia por asma
de los niños que nacerán con leucemia o lupus
todos los vientres de las madres espontáneamente
   abortivas
toda la tierra de siembra contaminada
todo el torrente de aguas y manantiales echados a perder

El día que murió Fidel
a mi país lo gobernaba
una Junta de Control Fiscal
jugábamos a las elecciones democráticas
sin rumbo o voluntad
todavía éramos colonia
vergonzoso territorio cabecibajo
poblado por valerosos luchadores que no luchan
   demasiado
que rinden honor al Norte
a su música, a su netflix, a su mcdonald, a su Trump

que alaban lo blanco y rubio
que gustan lo ojiazul
que anhelan el blackfriday y desdeñan las tribus nativas

El día que murió Fidel
Oscar López Rivera seguía bochornosamente preso
le componíamos poemas, canciones, cuentos
firmábamos peticiones de permiso al Imperio
nos comportábamos obedientes corderos
nadie orquestaba un plan de escape
un dinamitar la celda
un intercambio de balas en la huida
cantábamos el himno de oveja doblegada
criticábamos al cubano exiliado
no nos identificábamos con su alegría o su dolor
mofa a las celebraciones en la Havana
o de su luto, o de su duelo tempestivo

Pero
El día que murió Fidel
tú me besabas
yo te prometía abrazos en mis aureolas
tú me acenizabas la boca
un estertor orgásmico nos bautizaba etéreas
yo te bebía

tú me tragabas
nos juramos amnesia ante los meses perdidos
volvíamos a comenzar desde cero…

#ElDíaQueLiberaronAOscar

Vivo en un barrio
los maleantes le llaman Cacolina escucho gritos como
de celebración entre los vecinos
me encuentro decorando la ducha
cortina de baño nueva
los adornos son en blanco y rojo
dice: Love
deseo sorprender a mi esposa
yo
una mujer casada con otra
un principito casado con su zorra muestrario
de mariposas monarcas
lepidópteras naranjas
detalles de enamorada

entonces llama mi hermana Glory
pongo en pausa el canal de amazon music canción
Aguanile de Héctor Lavoe Glory entre lágrimas me
da la noticia
escuchar la frase
"Oscar es libre"
de sus labios
antes que de cualquier otra persona
ha sido un gran regalo

gracias a la vida
por haberme dado tanto

luego llamo a Zu
y lloramos

Eso estoy haciendo yo
el día que Obama concede la libertad
al Patriota Boricua Oscar López Rivera.

Guabancex

Voy a usar el nombre
lo usaré en tu escote
nombraré tu ombligo
caderas color carbón
Guabancex
tú, la única cemí hembra taína
incluida en la 'Relación acerca de las antigüedades
de los indios' de Fray Ramón Pané
tú Guabancex
y voy a convocarte
a saborearte
a diluirte
te bautizaré en el murmullo
y mi grito de posesión
seré Inriri Cahuvial
cual mito
cual Corretjer
seré cucubanos revoloteando sobre un espejo
seré una ráfaga que ya no era solo viento
seré dos alas, y con las unas, y con el pico del carpintero
te convertiré en deidad humana
en viento y agua indomable
brisa arremolinada que hace el hueco en mi vientre
de madera

yo también he taladrado tu perforación
la he punzado como un pájaro con pico en tu caoba
gloria a tus manos Guabancex
gloria a tu ira, a tus tormentas en mis senos
alabanza para nuestra boca patria
alabanza para nuestra lengua patria
nuestra beso patria
alabanza
seremos dos mujeres furiosas madres de Juracán
haremos un hijo en carne viva
seremos el río de Corozal, el de la leyenda dorada
haremos que la corriente arrastre oro, que la corriente
esté ensangrentada.

Decirte Gertrudis

déjame decirte Gertrudis
que tu osadía
tu enfrentamiento
tus letras
tu feminismo
tu valor
son fuera de este mundo

decirte que conformas mi constelación
de guerreras
cazadoras tribales pintadas
opuestas a la ablación
opuestas a la prima nocte
opuestas al macho cabrío
al himen como trofeo
al parto como mandato
eres valquiria a favor de la luz libertaria
que brinda el aborto a aquellas que así lo deseamos

déjame decirte Avellaneda
que tu abolicionismo da cátedra
se convierte en abrazo cálido
un batallar fiero en noche gélida
transmutación en sueño idealista

para que yo me libere
para que yo imprima valor a otras negras parejeras
como yo
a otras que serán gobernantes
presidentas del archipiélago de mi Isla
a quienes desollarán corruptos
yo pintaré mi rostro de amarillo guerrearé
cortaré cabezas
extirparé lenguas racistas
seré la Albizu
de un nuevo tiempo
seré Filiberta
seré la Oscar
me vuelvo yerbera
babalawo clitórica
santera con harem de hombres besadores
orgía de mujeres poliamorosas
espacio de creación
historial ancestral
polígama artivista
mercenaria afrodiaspórica
soldada africana de Dahomey
estratega negra de Benin
francotiradora de Senegal
amazona de Ghana
Anaïs Nin

Frida Khalo
Simone de Beauvoir
Sab
Carlota
Queen Nanny
Juana Agripina
Yo Makandal

las mujeres negras ancestrales de mi imperio mutilado
    y restituido
las mujeres librepensadoras de mi universo oprimido
    y rescatado
te saludan Gertrudis Gómez de Avellaneda.

Gloria

Gloria al Padre, Pedro Albizu Campos
Gloria al Hijo, Comandante Filiberto Ojeda Ríos
Gloria a la Trinidad y Espíritu Santa, Isabelita Rosado, Rafael Cancel Miranda y Lolita Lebrón
Como era en el principio, ahora y siempre, por los siglos de los siglos.
Ashé.

Letanías

Juana Agripina de Ponce
ruega por nosotras
negra Juana Díaz
ruega por nosotras
Mulata Soledad
ruega por nosotras
Carlota Lucumí de Cuba
ruega por nosotras
Queen Nanny de Jamaica
ruega por nosotras
Luiza Mahin de Brasil
ruega por nosotras
Guerrera Yennega
ruega por nosotras
Taytu Betul de Etiopía
ruega por nosotras
Nehanda Nyakasikana
rueguen por nosotras
Yaa Asantewaa reina Ashanti
ruega por nosotras
Nzinga Mbande de Angola
ruega por nosotras
Muhumusa de Uganda
ruega por nosotras

Sacerdotisa Kaigirwa
ruega por nosotras
Tarenorerer la negra de Australia
ruega por nosotras
soldadas de Dahomey
rueguen por nosotras
amazonas del reino de Benin
rueguen por nosotras
cimarronas de Borinken
rueguen por nosotras
amamantadoras de las Antillas
rueguen por nosotras
nodrizas y criadoras
rueguen por nosotras
negras paridoras
rueguen por nosotras
prietas vengadoras
rueguen por nosotras
Sojourner Truth
ruega por nosotras
Harriet Tubman
ruega por nosotras
Rosa Parks
ruega por nosotras
Assata Shakur
ruega por nosotras

Angela Davis
ruega por nosotras
Toussaint Louverture
ruega por nosotras
Saint-Domingue
ruega por nosotras
Ayití
ruega por nosotras
Puerto Rico
la tierra de Borinken donde he nacido yo
ruega por nosotras.

Bembetruenos

Y así le grito al villano:
yo sería borincana
aunque naciera en la luna;
también le grito que crecí
que lo superé, que me hice fuerte
que su acoso de llamar mi pelo malo
ya no agobia más, ya no duele, ya no taladra
que sus ofensas y agravios
pelo de alambre, boca de chopa
canto de negra, prieta apestosa
bemba grande, color de mierda
ya no me alcanzan;
que soy como la luna; soy del mar y soy montuna; que soy quimera en el canto
cristal del llanto; Puertorriqueña sin na, pero sin quebranto
soy Bembetrueno; más que un apodo de chica, más que un insulto sufrido
una mujer superhéroe luchadora por la identidad y la justicia
yo sería una orgullosa negra borincana
aunque naciera en la luna.

La señal de la Cruz

En el nombre de la bandera nacionalista negra que
es la Madre
y de la Hija, que es la cruz blanca en el medio
y en el Espíritu rebelde de la masacre de Ponce, calle
Aurora Domingo de Ramos
en donde cientos de banderas negras con cruces blancas
se tiñeron de rojo
cayeron al suelo y gobernó la impunidad
Amén.

Haitian Creole

Bonjou Atemis, Bondye fanm, Yemaya
Konplè nan Ashe
babalawo la rete nan mitan nou
beni pitit fi nou yo ki pran jistis nan men pwòp yo
ak Benediksyon pou fwi a nan oseyan Ochun ou

santa Yemaya
manman deyès
consentidora nan tout lanmou
nan tout lang ak nich nan bouch
chak fi ki renmen yon lòt fanm

Purisima Ave Yemayá
mete apa yo si nou ogmante pitit fi nou ak pitit gason
epi anseye yo fè grèv tounen bwè mari
maltratador
abizè
plen nan bal
ak lam
prete pou ekzekisyon

lapriyè pou mwen tou orishas
Obatala
Orula manman ak papa

bondye moun peyi ki apa pou èrmafrodit ak transganr
  zanj Bondye yo Eleguá
kounye a ak nan lè a
pou libète
dezobeyisans sivil
Defansè
livrezon nan peyi nou an
ak borincana drapo nou an
amèn

Yoruba

Kabiyesi Goddess, Yemaya
Full ti Ashe
awọn babalawo wà pẹlu nyin
sure fun awọn ọmọbinrin nyin ti o ya idajọ sinu ara wọn
ọwọ
ati ibukun ni awọn eso ti rẹ Oshun òkun

Santa Yemaya
iya orișa
consentidora ti gbogbo fẹ
ti gbogbo awọn ede ati swarms ti ète
gbogbo obinrin ti o fẹràn miran obinrin

Purisima Ave Yemayá
mimọ nipa igbega awọn ọmọbinrin wa ati awọn ọmọ
ki o si kọ wọn lati lu pada mu yó ọkọ
maltratador
abuser
ti o kún fun awako
ati abe
yawo fun ipaniyan

gbadura fun wa orishas
Obatala

Orula iya ati baba
awọn orișa awọn mimọ hermaphrodite ati transgender
    angẹli Eleguá
bayi ati ni wakati
ti ominira
abele aigboran
defenders
oba ti wa Ile-Ile
ati ki o wa flag borincana
Amin

De este mundo

Padre nuestro

Padre nuestro
que estuviste en la masacre de Orlando,
y que no hiciste nada
Santificado al mantenerte silente e inamovible por
las razones que todos tus seguidores conocen,
pero que el resto no. . .
Padre nuestro que suponemos consolando en este día
a los padres y madres de quienes perdieron sus vidas
esa noche. . .
Padre nuestro que te escondes en los cielos y que allí
permaneces, y quien desde allí haces creer que mandas
a buscar gente de la Tierra
dizque te hacen falta y por cuya razón son masacrados. . .
Padre nuestro que desde tu reino hechizas a tantos para
hacernos creer que todo es tu voluntad, que todo es tu

propósito, que nada pasa desapercibido ante ti y que somos tu creación imperfecta y poco racional ante tus designios. . .

Padre nuestro que me has visto besar de lengua a una mujer como yo, que conoces mi principio y mi final, mi origen y mi omega, mi alfa y mis orgasmos, mi urgencia sexual lesbiana

y la homosexual, bisexual, transexual, intersexual y pansexual de mis hermanos. . .

Santificada sea mi paciencia, tolerancia y aceptación para contigo, Padre.

En el nombre de los 49 fallecidos en la masacre de Pulse, en Orlando, que ojalá te perdonen, Amén.

No fui a recoger a mi hijo

no fui a recoger a mi hijo
como en el kínder
luego de hacer su lonchera
o a su espera en el merendero
velando que nadie lo molestara
cual primigenio padre ansioso
que necesita estar al frente de la verja
para verlo salir a salvo
estar ahí por si lo enfrenta un coloso
que lo hará llorar
que se burlará de sus músculos débiles
o de su vocecita de niña

no fui a reclamar a mi hijo
como cuando lo visitaba en el camerino
de su primera obra de teatro
o por su estreno en el cuerpo de bailarines
sabiendo que sufría
disimulando entre la canasta de frutas
alguna rosa escondida por su madre
aquellas que solo él disfrutaba en secreto
para evitar el acoso
la frustración

los miramientos y la humillación tosca
de tantos desentendidos

no fui a identificar a mi hijo
como en el desfile de la primera comunión
encubriendo su amistad con algún monaguillo
ocultando sus vestimentas coloridas
la maleta de maquillaje estrambótico
las pelucas, los sombreros y las estolas
las lentejuelas y los tacones en piel

no fui a cargar a mi hijo muerto
cual escultórica Pietà de Vaticano
no me atreví
no fui a su cuerpo
no fui a su rostro
ni a sus pestañas llorosas ante el dolor de los disparos
no fui a sus brazos temblorosos en la ausencia de mi
bendición
ni al hueco de cuello moribundo
al que le falta mi corona de flores
no vi sus labios pronunciando un lamento
no recité junto a su oreja el ángel de la guarda
no dije amén con él
no me retorcí ante su falta de pulso
ante su pestañear agónico

frente a su ultimo respiro
no quise estar ahí
no lo busqué en la morgue
no lo saqué de aquella nevera morada
no lo recogí para besar su frente
no lo enterré
tiene culpa la vergüenza
tiene culpa aquella discoteca
tiene culpa el asesino
tengo culpa yo
y en el fondo
no fui por el deseo de pensarlo aún vivo. . .

Ley 54

no cantemos victoria
reconocer tu violencia
y mi victimización
no es prodigio

saber que ahora
es lícita la llegada de la policía
para ayudarme
para encarcelarte
volverme víctima oficial
mártir legal

testificar frente a fantoches
de un mequetrefe sistema
una parodia isleña
que entona embracetada
yo sería borincano aunque naciera en la luna
mientras espera con paciencia
por washington
y su limosna igualitaria
no tiene nada de glamoroso. . .
no cantemos victoria

Escala sismológica

mi mano diversa
mi puño diverso
mi brazo diverso
variación de colores
y de una bandera

confieso amar a una mujer
a sus pechos redondos y abultados
o caídos con la hidalguía de los años
confieso enloquecer con sus pezones

ante esto
el vigor de mis delitos
frente a cualquier cristo
es menor a 3.2

confieso instigar
la consecución de un aguerrido fellatio
mientras practico la inmoralidad de un cunnilingus
en una mezcla de aromas amorosos
triángulo atípico
cuya dimensión asciende a moderada: 5.6

si exteriorizo fantasear
con la intelectual y sexy Lizza Fernanda
sus formas carnales
sus axiomas verbales
su elocución
el sismo aumenta los oleajes: 7.3

si por el contrario
gimo
vocifero
clamo
retrueno
retumbo
desato
y grito a la memoria de Jorge Steven
la devastación causará graves daños
mi denuncia
se convierte en evento
nunca antes registrado
mi ira destruye a intolerantes
a los odiadores biblia en mano
a los asesinos imitadores de caín
y la historia humana
jamás habrá inscrito
indignación
de tal magnitud

la ira es así de intensa
pero el amor es otra cosa

y hace tiempo que tú y yo
no pertenecemos a esta escala

Mapa al clítoris

lo primero que se requiere es esto:
manos inocentes
lavadas en la sangre del cordero
y el animalito queda por la ingle
o enjuagadas con la savia
de la oveja menstruante

lo segundo
se requiere que seas católica
apostólica o romana
mariana
carismática o adventista
mormona
atalaya o pentecostal
seguidora de kardec
orisha
wica
babalawo o pagana

que seas algo de eso
y también tímida
o seductora
femenina o tosca
no importa, da igual

prometo sacarte del clóset
frente a abuelos
hermanos, hermanas
tías políticas
vecinos bochincheros
y primos que se exprimen

seré tu primera
tu conquistadora
la inolvidable
y te entregaré la cartografía exacta
para que llegues
mapa a un clítoris bien lamido
gustosamente succionado

no te perderás nunca
por esas avenidas
¡prometido!
y podrás otorgar
las correctas direcciones
de todo cuanto se goza
a la siguiente

Poema a Wanda

¿alguna vez sentiste, wanda
el tremor de la boca
que se posa en la cúspide
de un glande femenino?

nosotras también tenemos
ese promontorio

esa nube de carne
centro de palpitaciones
del kléitos, klitos, cleitós
palabra griega, wanda
instrúyete

lamer un labio inferior, wanda
y pensarlo en fenicio
pensarlo en latín o en arameo
pensarlo desde la etimología
recreada para comunicar cosas
acercarnos con esa interacción
y temblarnos
trepidarte

succionar la pequeña colina
y traer a la memoria
la academia de la lengua de cualquier país
subir a lamer la lengua de cualquier mujer
o mejor aún
las papilas gustativas de la mujer que se ama
seguir al pie de la letra
las palabras del diccionario
un libro verdaderamente venerable

real
academia
real academia
palabra
verbo que se hace carne
y habita entre nosotras
letras santificadas
más sagradas que las del otro libro
que tergiversas

¿sabes tú dónde queda ese botón
que nos hace estallar, wanda
alguien
alguna vez te lo ha activado?

¿algún hombre
alguna mujer
algún hombre que parezca mujer
alguna mujer que parezca hombre
o algún hermano intersexual
de vagina y pene?

¿te han mostrado cómo se ordeñan
las melosas ubres
de una mujer excitada, wanda
te explicó tu papá
lo que era masturbarse
o te habló tu madre
de las virtudes de permanecer virgen por el frente
mientras entregas las nalgas aceitadas?

¿te contaron de la delicia
de no saber distinguir
entre ano y vulva
sabes tú cómo se aromatiza
una vagina menstruante?

anticrística wanda
patética apóstol
de la nueva inquisición
¡de cuanto te pierdes!

Oubao Moin Rosa

Celebración de una leyenda multicolor
Celebración de una corriente y arco iris
Celebración y otro crimen de odio
¡Alabanza!

Amanecemos agonizantes con otro Jorge Steven
Amanecemos llorosos y expectantes
Amanecemos con ramas que chorrean sangre
¡Alabanza!

El negro, la india, el jabao,
la blanca, el mulato, el trigueño quiebran sus hombros
Los cuerpos marcan el carimbo del triángulo rosa
Y sigue el horror y el abuso
¡Alabanza!

Gloria a esas manos lesbianas que trabajan.
Gloria a esas manos homosexuales que trabajan.
Gloria a esas manos bisexuales que trabajan.
¡Alabanza!

Gloria a esas manos transexuales que trabajan.
Gloria a esas manos transgéneros.
Gloria a esas manos diversas.

Porque ellas la patria amasan.
¡Alabanza!

¡La patria de todas las manos!
Para ellas y para su patria, ¡Alabanza!, ¡Alabanza!
Manos rosadas que construyen y saldrán de ellas la nueva patria liberada.

Lugares públicos

"Your silence will not protect you."

—Audre Lorde

Soy una pata respetuosa
las muestras de afecto
me las guardo para el decoro del colchón

así dicta nuestro credo y hay que ser estrictos
no besuquear a otra mujer en público
nada de enclavar la lengua entre sus labios
como el anclaje de lancha
sobre el mar de Cayo Caracoles
ni masajear con la puntita sus encías
agua cristalina en Isla Caja de Muertos
mucho menos cerrar los ojos
apretar su cintura
dejarme apretar por ella
timones o pedaleos en el alambique
en La Parguera o El Faro
ni escurrir las manos más allá de la espalda
ni meter los dedos en su alcancía de carne
así como si bailáramos una balada de marquesina
en un balneario de Dorado o Isla Verde
o una bachata a pleno sol

como hacen los novios o los adúlteros
aquellos que se quieren

Soy una negra respetuosa
que el deseo de escribir
sobre verdades y opresiones
jamás me lleve a señalar al blanco
o a sus abuelos
aquellos que seguramente esclavizaron a los míos
nada de querer mejorar la raza
o atrasarla
nada de poemas de igualdad
ni de versos sobre el prejuicio
no hay que molestar a los nietos
quienes heredaron el status quo
con recuerdos mentirosos

habrá que alizar el pelo
nada de afros encaracoladitos
habré de desteñir la piel
evitar el suntan de playa Piñones a cualquier precio

hay que respetar a los no oprimidos
a los que nunca lo han estado
sea usted una negra respetable
una pata digna y moral

disculpa
¿te ofende rememorar el cadalso
el cepo, los latigazos
la metida de pene blanco
en todas las vaginas negras?
perdona por recordarlo
a ti que te has esforzado tanto por olvidar

¿te ofende nuestro beso
mientras escondes tu homofobia
tras una película porno sobre lesbianas?
¡cuanta insensibilidad de mi parte!

mis excusas
olvido que para tu tranquilidad
crees que no metemos mano

repito mi credo
hay que ser estrictos
no olvide ser blanca
lo más blanca posible
no olvide comportarse como hetero
lo más hetero posible
de usted se espera el mejor comportamiento
en lugares públicos
no lo reniegue

no instruya a aquellos que no cuestionan
aquellos que no leen
a los que no saben su historia y no la quieren saber
a quienes desean permanecer necios o ignorantes
que defienden la no lucha por aparentar
por parecer blanco
o heterosexual
que al final viene siendo lo mismo

Confieso

propuesta de matrimonio a Zulma

Confieso que escribo poemas en las páginas en blanco
de los libros de narrativa y luego las arranco
Confieso que no tengo pintadas todas las uñas
de mis pies y qué me gusta andar en chancletas
confieso que tengo 148 versiones del libro El Principito
una en árabe que no entiendo
otra en húngaro
alemán, italiano, portugués, francés y hasta varias
pirateadas
Confieso que tengo un principito tatuado en el pezón
de mi oscura teta derecha
Confieso que eso es una mentira;
el tatuaje reposa en mi hombro izquierdo
Confieso que juré jamás volver a casarme
y ahora que pronto se podrá celebrar la igualdad
lo haré con una mujer a la que nunca le he pedido
matrimonio
Confieso que me gusta su boca
el olor de su cuello y el juego que hacen nuestros dos aros
comprometidos
ella y yo somos un libro en blanco en el que habremos de
escribir

cuentos y poemas de alto contenido erótico
Confieso que nunca me he arrodillado frente a nadie
y que ésta será la primera vez...
Así que Zulma
Mi adorada
Tú que eres la Zorra de mi Principito
¿Quieres casarte conmigo?

Perigeo

Bésame el perigeo
este ombligo de olas desbordadas
que te bendicen el rostro
Tómame por el ángulo que más cerca quede a tu boca
y atrapa esta garganta con tu mano cerrada
con tu mordida de labios lunares
Ata las cuerdas
Desplázame en este jardín de feromonas
que gotean
cual rosas transformadas en océanos
inundando tus pieles jadeantes
Hazme tu Superluna
Vuélveme tu órbita y seca la marea de estos ojos
que tanto te han llorado
Desviste este cráter
y alunízame los pliegues profundos
esos que bombean sangre
que palpitan tempestad ante tu regreso.

Dos iguales

poema invitación a la boda masiva 2015

Amarse entre dos iguales
en el fragor de una pasión entre mujer y mujer
entre hombre y hombre
abrazar mientras llega el momento justo
vociferar a los cuatro vientos que ya es hora
este es nuestro momento...

nos provoca ser una misma carne
queremos prometernos cosquillas, desayunos, vacaciones
deseamos jurarnos gentilezas, lágrimas de felicidad,
ternuras...

Soy la primicia de la vid
Tú la cosecha de agave
Ambas somos un atardecer
frente al mar del Morro
Ambos somos un abrazo
con esencia a café y tembleque
dos comisuras de labios
dos ramos de pestañas
el deseo apasionado por pronunciar
en nuestra Isla del Encanto

"Yo te amo; yo acepto ser tu esposo"
"Yo te adoro; yo acepto ser tu esposa".

Familiares, amigos y allegados de Puerto Rico
los invitamos a que sean parte de nuestra unión legal
nuestra liberación, nuestra equidad y nuestra justicia
el domingo 19 de julio de 2015, a la 1:00 pm
en el Viejo San Juan

¿Dónde están las almohadas?

«alea iacta est»

Qué necesitas para ser feliz, preguntas
ilusionada contesto:
una amante que me regale almohadas

una almohada suave y firme
con memoria de látex o foam
para recordar lo estrictamente necesario
y olvidar que no tengo anillo

una almohada de plumas
antialergénica y sin asma
para dormir de lado
volar boca arriba
cruzar mi piel con otra piel
en la certeza que alguien me entienda
carente de psicoanálisis

una almohada que no lleve al límite
ni me diagnostique
que entienda la ecuación de Einstein
la radiación de Hawkings
las once dimensiones

una casa construida en Kepler
el vicio del teclado

una almohada para que mi cuello
quede hermosamente horizontal
alineado con el resto de la desconfiada columna
postura vertebral herida
por las promesas a medias
o el dolor abierto
tan espantosamente abierto
sin esperanza de redención

Quienes duermen de lado
suelen requerir sueños y besos de boca franca
silbido de lengua sexy
lágrimas y mocos que no ahoguen al convocarlos;
se sugiere almohadas más gruesas
con una disculpa a tiempo
que no te saque en cara errores pasados
ni el día en que fuiste víctima y no victimario

Una almohada blanda y fina
que te haga dormir boca abajo
puede evitar lo que dicta la terapia fría
aquellas que hospitalizan el agravio
en contra de los apapuchos

las consecuencias de una postura inadecuada
traerá falta de descanso y olvido
rigidez de cuello
contracturas en la mañana
o hasta finales azarosos;
si te mueves mucho y cambias de postura
una almohada de firmeza media
será desagradecida
no valorará tus esfuerzos
te hará llorar durante los tapones
mientras te cepillas los dientes frente al espejo
y en el baño de damas de la oficina
así irás perdiendo la cabeza
y roncarás grandilocuentemente loca

Me hice madre

celebración del Día de las Madres 2015

Me hice madre el día que pujé tus enjambres de
piel acojinada que pesaron siete con seis en octubre.
Me hice madre con tu extensión saliéndoseme cuan
larga y misericordiosa en el sillón de tus veintiuna
pulgadas; manos de agarre de pulgares míos, piernas
de patadas como tambora en mi ombligo, retumbe de
estrías dibujadas en mi tronco cual si fueras mujer
homoerectus enhebrando imágenes dentro de una
caverna occipital; mi útero edénico y prehistórico
ahora bautizado en la bendición de tu tránsito.
Me hice madre en la garganta, cuando te vi y me
miraste, cuando esos ojos de asteroide principesco se
clavaron en los míos y yo me ahogué en la intensidad
de tu maestría, de tu dominio, de la conquista que
demostrabas ya tener sobre mí, en tan sólo esos
primeros veintiún segundos de vida. Palpitaste y me
declaraste Entera. Me convertí en bólido de Oriónidas.
Rajaste mi línea cubital con destreza aguerrida para
que a partir de ese momento yo te defendiera, yo te
amparara, yo te declarara Única, Potente, Feroz. Eso
eres, una hija feroz que me ha convertido en la madre

más llena de gracia de la galaxia. Soy tuya, aurora boreal, desde ese día y hasta el por siempre.

A mi hija Aurora

Constancia así

Constancia así
en certeza de espejo
de saberme enlazada con tu nombre
de saberte no sola
y a mí más amigable
en esta edad corta que te mira
que ya sabe tu borrachera
caídas tristonas
tropiezos alegres
el cantazo
choque de esquina con la realidad
porque extrañas a un hombre
como extrañaré yo a una mujer
cuando crezca
no ahora;
no bajo este cielo nublado
a punto de nieve
en el que ambas somos extranjeras
y nos hemos encontrado
un callejón fétido
soy Constancia
una niña que persevera
y ese empeño tuyo de sonreírme
en un barrio que no te pertenece

que no es de ti ni de mí
que no habla como tú
o como yo

tenaces
estuvimos de acuerdo en jugar
o estuve de acuerdo yo
porque tú ibas muy mareada
debutante sobre el suelo
algunos vómitos agrestes
la violencia del buche masticado
basurero de grosellas
insolencia de aceras
paredes añejadas en el miedo

yo también ando escondida
huyendo al padrastro
dolerte aquí
en este callejón protector
de ojos bozales recolectando algodones
qué te duele misi, dónde te hinca
justo en medio de mi pueblo dormido

jugamos al san serení
a la buena, buena vida
hacen así, así los escritores

así, así, así
así me gusta a mí

y dijiste que eras poeta
te regalé mi nombre:
haga una poesía, misi
con la palabra Constanza
que así me llamo
así también te llamas tú
mi segundo nombre, comentaste
porque el primero es Julia

y trataste de ponerte en pie
quitándote las colillas de cigarro
de la cabeza
intentaste doblar la pierna
apoyarte
balancear la caneca
botella de cristal soberbio
anestesiante de turcas
desenamoradas

ay ay ay—dijiste—que eres grifa
y pura negra
señalaste mis cabellos
grifería en pelo

acariciaste mi boca
cafrería en labios
y tu chata nariz es nuestra

qué te lastima misi, dónde te punza
en el hombre, negra linda—susurraste
me duele el hombre
dolerte aquí
justo en medio de tu abuelo esclavo
justo en medio de los opresores
vergüenza si hubiese sido amo
ay, ay, ay

Julia rebelde

Guerrera te llaman las olas
del mar que te bañan...

fuiste Jane Doe
por poco tiempo
eres y siempre serás hasta la eternidad
subversiva marejada grande de Loíza
una revoltosa indomable
mujer de valores
que quiero repetir en mí
en mis hijas
en las hijas de mis hijas

amalgama de rebeliones eres
un puñado de saetas apalabradas eres
una confabuladora
con Albizu
Corretjer
Martí
Juan Bosch
tu nombre aparece en los archivos del FBI
tu nombre aparece en los archivos del FBI
cartas que devolvieron la conciencia eres
un bólido de sensatez

letras que impulsan el furor
que humilla a los tibios

Y tienes la noble hidalguía de la hermana España
Y el fiero cantillo taíno bravío, lo tienes también

«Bendito el día en que sea una mujer
la que caiga defendiendo la libertad de su patria
Ese día habrá una revolución
en cada hogar puertorriqueño
y se reconocerá en pleno
la grandeza de nuestra justa causa»

Palabras de una insigne Julia en 1936
carimbos indelebles de huella temeraria
la Julia rebelde
la Julia estoica
la Julia que me gusta homenajear
mujer indómita
desobediente
mujer que quema las ansias
de ser aguerrido y audaz capitán
mujer que sería un obrero
picando la caña, sudando el jornal

ya las gentes murmuran
que eres Patria completa
que se alza en versos
no en tu voz: en mi voz

Guerrera te llaman los bardos que versan tu historia
No importa el tirano te trate con blanca maldad
Poeta serás con bandera, con lauros y gloria
Rebelde, Gran Julia, te llaman las hijas de la libertad.

Soy Julia y he regresado

Soy Julia y he regresado a nacer
el 17 de febrero
he regresado Amanecida
a acunarme en la Canción de la verdad sencilla
he vuelto Casi al Alba a amarte Juan Isidro
pero no pienso perseguirte hasta La Habana
no te daré mis manos ni mis uñas clavadas a tu espalda
no te adornaré de besos ni de pasiones el cuello
no permitiré que me entregues tan solo
un boleto de ida
me envíes a Nueva York sin un ultimátum
ante el temor de que tu madre o tu padre no te quieran
conmigo

Soy Julia, Julia negra
que soy grifa y pura prieta
y he regresado a decirte Juan Isidro
que no vale la pena emborracharse por ti
o por si tu esposa te deja
o por si te quedas con ella
o por si pierdes toda tu herencia

Yo Soy Julia, Juan Isidro
y mi Río Grande de Loíza en esta vuelta

no será dedicado a tus contornos
seré la Julia que quiere ser hombre
que quiere ser capitán del barco Pentacromía
seré la Julia que conocerá a Sor Juana y a Sor Filotea
aquella qué quiere invitar a salir a todos los hombres que
    me dé la gana
mientras batallo
con boricuas valerosas que cuidan su Isla
que pelean por su autonomía, por su soberanía y por la
    decisión de ser yo soy Julia
aquella que ha fundado el ejército Hijas de la Libertad
aquella que ha compuesto poemas
y escrito libros coqueteando a Corretjer
soy la Julia de Burgos que agradece a los maestros
el enseñar con perspectiva de género
aunque no existan cartas circulares o huecas
    reglamentaciones
soy la Julia que no quiere que haya niñas
que se sientan menos que un niño
la que quiere que las jovencitas aspiren ser todo
    lo que anhelan
soy la Julia que desea lo mejor para la patria
la Julia del Poema con la tonada última
Poema de la cita eterna
Poema de la íntima agonía
Poema de mi pena dormida

Poema del hijo no nacido
Poema para las lágrimas
Proa de mi velero de ansiedad
Poema para mi muerte

Soy Julia de Burgos
Y en este regreso te conozco Yolanda de mí
eres verso entre mis labios, negra parejera
eres El Viaje Alado
las Velas de un recuerdo
conmigo has sido Yo misma fui mi ruta
conmigo eres la más callada

Yo Soy Julia Constancia
y en este regreso no he muerto en las calles
de ningún barrio anglosajón
no he padecido pulmonía
el frío no cala mis huesos
por haber estado tirada en la acera
no hay nieve
no hay hielo

Soy Julia de Burgos de Arroyo Pizarro de Oliveras Vega y
de Cruz Bernal
soy la que exige: Dadme mi número
Ya

Carne negra

oler carne negra sangre negra/ morder negrura/
pellizcar negros cachetes/ trastear tus negras nalgas /
recordar a mami ennegrecida/ oscurantizada / tiznada
de carbones briosos/canturrear nanas negras de mi
negro abuelo coco / tembleque negro / majarrete
tosco / toco toto toco toto vejigante come toto /
marrayo negrísimo en boca rayada / bembes negrotes
pa' morderte en piñones/ pestañas noctámbulas
de singarte en cataño/ costa isla de cabras / costa
punta salinas/ costa perla/ costa boca bemba / arete
de argolla prieta/ nariz criolla mulata y marrón / te
ennegrezco el ojal del chupete trigueño/ ennegréceme
la lengua violeta cafre/ acaríciame la encía púrpura
con negrete dulce / trucutá trucutá/ tu negra cebolla /
trucutá trucutá/ tu negra pinga negra / tan buena que
está tu dulcísima profundidad soterrada / el cepeda
y el ayala en cada espasmo / consiénteme en la libre
plena / en la bomba suelta/ en el dulce e coco/ negrita
linda/ una crica azul/ oscurísima / toda tuya / negra
tuya / tan buena que está /pizarro soy

Bravado

Italia, 2016

Tu boca
una orquesta que dirige inconsistencias
y que aprende nuevos modos
de arrebatar la sanidad
si una imagina
el incendio musical de tu embestida
o el escalofrío sonoro
en el que nace toda mi locura

Desde aquel beso profundo
ensalivado con la miel de tu lunar de rostro
te veo volver. . .
colocar la insignia
plantar bandera entre rosas azules
apretar los colmillos en mi cuello ofrenda

Tu boca
un arrecife abatido por cocteles molotov
si el sonido exigente de tu arribo
brama en los tonos del piano
aulla en las cuerdas del violoncello
muge enterrando los ritmos del claroscuro

Mientras aluniza el crescendo de tu conquista
cual emperador romano
cual Alejandro Magno
la mia ragazza, la mia donna, dolce fidanzata
tus labios bajos y contraltos
regalan el Bravado exquisito
la postura
el contorno
la soberanía de una mandíbula
recorrido altanero de tu ejército
ante el mapamundi de mi piel

Y truenas
vociferas
como criatura primitiva
que restrega la cabeza en mi mollera
mordiendo el lenguaje de los homínidos;
desencajadas ambas
sumergidas en el éxtasis de un amanecer derramado

#OccupyMe

Soy octubreriana, octubrerina, octubrina, octuberista. Escribo únicamente los días 29. Menstrúo cabalgada en el asteroide b612 próximo a colisionar con el planeta. Agonizo cansada de injusticias, de exclusiones, harta de las diferencias—todas ellas inventadas. Por eso escribo. Susurro la palabra desosirio en la boca del Principito. Un susurro-denuncia, un diseño cuántico ancestral en donde los paralelos, los agujeros negros y las supernovas me dan el perfecto derecho de besar la boca de hombres y mujeres, parir criaturas con vulva desde mi vulva, y tararear canciones de Calle 13.

Soy una mujer que ocupa, una negra que ocupa, una bisexual que ocupa. Soy la denunciadora interventora que troca, que transgrede, que invierte. Piel oscura, ojos brujos, pestañas enredaderas. Puertorriqueña con 29 lunares en todo el cuerpo, un mapa gitanesco en cada palma de la mano y poco aire en los pulmones, por asmática. Soy el sexo opuesto del sexo opuesto, a quien toca su mismo espejo. He sido parida en novilunio por mi unigénita de nombre austral.

Por eso escribo.

YOLANDA ARROYO PIZARRO es escritora puertorriqueña. Ha publicado libros que denuncian y visibilizan apasionados enfoques que promueven la discusión de la afroidentidad y la sexodiversidad. Es Directora del Departamento de Estudios Afropuertorriqueños, un proyecto performático de Escritura Creativa con sede en la Casa Museo Ashford, en San Juan, PR y ha fundado la Cátedra de Mujeres Negras Ancestrales, jornada que responde a la convocatoria promulgada por la UNESCO de celebrar el Decenio Internacional de los Afrodescendientes. Ha sido invitada por la ONU al Programa "Remembering Slavery" para hablar de mujeres, esclavitud y creatividad en 2015. Su libro de cuentos *las Negras*, ganador del Premio Nacional de Cuento PEN Club de Puerto Rico en 2013, explora los límites del devenir de personajes femeninos que desafían las jerarquías de poder. *Caparazones*, *Lesbofilias* y *Violeta* son algunas de sus obras que exploran la transgresión desde el lesbianismo abiertamente visible. La autora ha ganado también el Premio del Instituto de Cultura Puertorriqueña en 2015 y 2012, y el Premio Nacional del Instituto de Literatura Puertorriqueña en 2008. Ha sido traducida al alemán, francés, italiano, inglés, portugués y húngaro.

ALEJANDRO ÁLVAREZ NIEVES Escritor, traductor y profesor. Ha publicado los poemarios *El proceso traductor* (Libros AC, 2012) y *Quiebre de Armas* (Trabalis Editores, 2018), además de la colección de cuentos *Galería de comandos* (Ediciones Alayubia, 2019). De 2011 a 2016, fungió como coordinador de escritores del Festival de la Palabra, organizado en San Juan por Mayra Santos Febres y José Manuel Fajardo, para luego convertirse en programador general hasta 2018. Ha traducido para varias revistas literarias como *World Poetry* y *Poetry Review,* así como editoriales internacionales como Temas de Hoy. Su traducción al español de *Wild Beauty, Belleza salvaje,* de Ntozake Shange (Atria Books, 2017), le mereció en premio International Latino Book Award en 2018, en la categoría de traducción al español. Alejandro Álvarez Nieves es catedrático auxiliar en el Programa Graduado de Traducción de la Universidad de Puerto Rico, Recinto de Río Piedras.

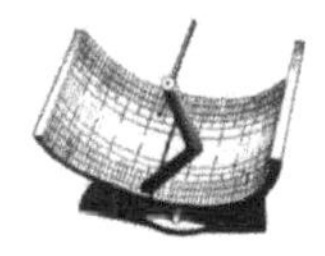

Milton Keynes UK
Ingram Content Group UK Ltd.
UKHW051133250324
439991UK00005B/511